This couldn't

She couldn't let it h
destroyed her bef
stand no chance of

Alison closed her eyes so that she couldn't see the expression in those tantalising green eyes, wishing as she waited for Grant to release her that she could also shut down her sense of smell as she caught the once so familiar male scent of him.

Dear Reader

Autumn books to warm the heart! Gideon really believes he has NOTHING LEFT TO GIVE until Beth proves him wrong, in Caroline Anderson's latest story. Their past relationship makes Alison and Grant decide to be STRICTLY PROFESSIONAL in work, according to Laura MacDonald. Abigail Gordon's CALMER WATERS and Judith Ansell's HIS SHELTERING ARMS are equally touching. We think you'll love these stories.

The Editor

!!!STOP PRESS!!! If you enjoy reading these medical books, have you ever thought of writing one? We are always looking for new writers for LOVE ON CALL, and want to hear from you. Send for the guidelines, with SAE, and start writing!

Laura MacDonald lives in the Isle of Wight. She is married and has a grown-up family. She has enjoyed writing fiction since she was a child, but for several years she worked for members of the medical profession, both in pharmacy and in general practice. Her daughter is a nurse and has helped with the research for Laura's medical stories.

Recent titles by the same author:

TO LOVE AGAIN
FALSE IMPRESSIONS

STRICTLY PROFESSIONAL

BY
LAURA MACDONALD

MILLS & BOON

MILLS & BOON LIMITED
ETON HOUSE, 18-24 PARADISE ROAD
RICHMOND, SURREY TW9 1SR

DID YOU PURCHASE THIS BOOK WITHOUT A COVER?
If you did, you should be aware it is **stolen property** as it was reported *unsold and destroyed* by a retailer. Neither the Author nor the publisher has received any payment for this book.

All the characters in this book have no existence outside the imagination of the Author, and have no relation whatsoever to anyone bearing the same name or names. They are not even distantly inspired by any individual known or unknown to the Author, and all the incidents are pure invention.

All Rights Reserved. The text of this publication or any part thereof may not be reproduced or transmitted in any form or by any means, electronic or mechanical, including photocopying, recording, storage in an information retrieval system, or otherwise, without the written permission of the publisher.

This book is sold subject to the condition that it shall not, by way of trade or otherwise, be lent, resold, hired out or otherwise circulated without the prior consent of the publisher in any form of binding or cover other than that in which it is published and without a similar condition including this condition being imposed on the subsequent purchaser.

MILLS & BOON, the Rose Device and LOVE ON CALL are trademarks of the publisher.

First published in Great Britain 1994 by Mills & Boon Limited

© Laura MacDonald 1994

Australian copyright 1994   Philippine copyright 1994 This edition 1994

ISBN 0 263 78830 X

Set in Times 10 on 12 pt.

03-9410-42584

Made and printed in Great Britain

CHAPTER ONE

'PLEASE, God, don't let anything happen to him.'

Alison Kennedy stood on the upper deck as the ferry edged closer to the familiar coastline of the Isle of Wight.

'You must go at once.' Dr Diana Richards, senior partner of the Suffolk practice where Alison had recently completed her GP training, had been emphatic when the news had come through.

It was unthinkable that anything should happen to her father, thought Alison; he was such a vital man, active, and as far as she could remember hadn't had a day's illness in his life. In fact it had been his boast that he'd never missed a surgery at his own Isle of Wight practice.

'A heart attack,' Grant Ashton, her father's partner, had told her over the phone, and as she'd clutched the receiver in disbelief he'd added, 'I think you'd better come home right away.'

As she thought of Grant her hands instinctively tightened on the ship's rail, her knuckles showing white, while the playful April breeze loosened tendrils of her long dark hair, whipping them across her face. For a long time now she had deliberately chosen a time to visit when she knew Grant Ashton was away on leave —skiing in Austria or on one of his sailing trips to France—but this time he would be there; this time she knew there would be no avoiding him.

And when moments later the ferry edged into Yarmouth harbour he was there, waiting for her, his tall figure leaning against the bonnet of his car. Even from that distance she could see his face, the expression grim, unsmiling, and although she knew he'd seen her at the rail he made no attempt to raise his hand in greeting.

She swallowed and turned away, for one moment blinking back angry tears as she stared back across the Solent at white furrows of foam in the wake of the ferry.

As she came through the terminal he was waiting for her at the entrance. The dark hair still fell over his forehead in the way she remembered and the greenish eyes were narrowed against the bright sunlight. He was wearing a well-cut, stone-coloured jacket and trousers, and she guessed he must be on call.

For a moment they stared at each other. Still there was no smile of welcome and Alison scanned the grim features for some sign, some flicker of reassurance.

'How is he?' she spoke at last.

'Fighting.'

She drew in her breath sharply. 'Where?'

'The hospital. I'll take you there.'

Wordlessly she allowed him to take her bags, followed him through the crowd of passengers to the car, watched as he stowed her luggage in the boot of the dark green BMW, then, as he opened the door for her, mechanically slid into the passenger seat.

They barely spoke on the twelve-mile drive to the hospital, but as Grant brought the car to a halt in the car park and she fumbled with the door-catch she felt his hand on her arm. For one moment she froze, unable to bring herself to speak or even to look at him, then in a low voice he said, 'It isn't good, Alison.'

She remained very still for a further moment then, as if suddenly galvanised into action, she opened the door, scrambled from the car and without a backward glance hurried across the car park.

She found him in the coronary care unit—at least the card above his bed stated that the patient was Miles Kennedy, but the unconscious, ashen-faced figure wired to a heart monitor bore little resemblance to her beloved father.

For the rest of that day and most of the night she sat beside him, holding his hand, hoping he knew she was there, her own training forgotten as she desperately looked to the medical team to work some miracle.

He died a little after two o'clock and as Alison, numb with shock, allowed the sister to lead her from the room she found Grant waiting for her.

His arms folded around her as he held her wordlessly and, in spite of the depth of her grief, the unexpected familiarity of his nearness brought some measure of comfort.

He drove her home to Woodbridge, the small town near Yarmouth, and to Fairacre, the large black and white gabled house where she had been brought up, where the brass plaque beside the door stated that Miles Kennedy and Grant Ashton were in partnership.

In spite of the hour they were met by Hilda Lloyd, who kept house for the two men and who had been at Fairacre for as long as Alison could remember. In dressing-gown and slippers, her white hair in rollers, Hilda hovered anxiously in the hallway as they let themselves into the house. One glance at their faces must have told her all she needed to know and her rosy face crumpled.

'Oh, Alison, my poor child.' Hilda opened her arms and gathered Alison to her as if she were still the child she had once cared for.

The nightmare of the next few days was mercifully dulled by shock and, as if in a daze, Alison did all that was expected of her. Hilda continued to run Fairacre as she had always done and Grant Ashton kept the surgeries going, somehow managing with the help of a nearby practice to care for Miles Kennedy's patients as well as his own.

Alison slept in her old room at the back of the house, the room under the gables that looked out over the fields to the estuary. She found some comfort in the familiar surroundings but she ached for her father, an ache that was physical, that lay heavy in her chest waiting to be relieved by tears that would not come. On the day before the funeral she took herself out of the house and walked for miles along the causeway that ran parallel to the estuary, a walk she'd done so many times with her father.

On her return she approached the house from the rear, avoiding the busy front entrance that the patients used. Crossing the lawn, she slipped into the sitting-room through the French doors that stood open to the spring sunshine, then wandered down the passage to the kitchen.

Hilda looked up from the table where she was preparing vegetables for the evening meal. 'Hello, love, I wondered where you'd got to.'

'I went for a walk.' Alison sighed, then restlessly crossed the room, took a blue and white mug from the dresser and poured herself a coffee from the pot that constantly bubbled on the Aga. 'Have you seen Dr Ashton?' She sat on a stool and curled her hands around her mug, drawing comfort from the warmth. She hadn't felt really warm since she'd heard of her father's attack.

Hilda glanced up, her vegetable knife poised. 'Not since lunch—why?'

Alison shrugged. 'I think he might have gone to the hospital—I was wondering if they've done the post-mortem yet.'

Hilda's eyes clouded over. 'It was so sudden. I still can't believe it, Alison. One moment he was in his room taking surgery, the next—well, the ambulance was here and he was on his way to hospital...'

'I know, Hilda...I know.'

Hilda wiped the back of one hand across her eyes. 'Dr Ashton has been marvellous—I don't know how he's managed to keep everything going.' She sniffed. 'But he'll have to have some help soon—there's no way he can keep going on his own.'

'He's probably waiting until the funeral is over then he'll arrange to get a locum,' Alison replied slowly.

Hilda was silent for a moment, carefully dicing a swede while Alison watched her, then she looked up.

'What about you, love?' she asked anxiously at last.

'Me?'

'Yes, how have you been? We don't see so much of you these days.'

Alison gave a slight shrug and gazed down into the depths of her mug. 'I've been very busy, Hilda.'

'Have you enjoyed your training year?'

'Oh, yes, very much.' She paused, reflecting, then added, 'I enjoyed my hospital training as well but I always wanted to be a GP, you know that.'

Hilda nodded, hesitated, then said. 'So what happens now that your training is over—will you be leaving Suffolk?'

'Not immediately—I'm doing locum for the practice at the moment and there's a chance I might stay. One of the partners is coming up for retirement—they've already indicated they would like me as his replacement.'

'Would you want that, dear?'

Alison shrugged and put her mug down. 'I may do —I'm very happy there.' She paused and glanced at Hilda and, noticing the older woman's speculative glance, she stood up and stretched. 'I think I'll go and see if Dr Ashton is back yet.' Suddenly she had to get away from Hilda, away from the look in her eyes. She felt guilty really, knew she should stay and talk to Hilda, knew Hilda would be concerned about what would happen at Fairacre now. But she couldn't, not yet. She knew the future had to be faced, decisions had to be made, but for the moment she could only live one day at a time; the funeral had to be lived through, that was the top priority, but first she needed to know why her father had died.

She made her way to the front of the house where

patients were already arriving for the early evening surgery. Gill, the practice secretary, was typing in her office and Sue, the receptionist, was sorting patient records. Alison leaned across the reception desk. 'Sue, is Dr Ashton in?'

'Yes, he's just got back.' The girl nodded.

'Does he have a patient with him?'

'No, he hasn't started surgery yet.'

'In that case I'll just go and have a word with him.'

'He has a full surgery.' The girl looked faintly accusing.

'I won't keep him a moment.' As she spoke Alison crossed the reception hall and entered the new wing of the building that had been added to Fairacre when Grant Ashton had gone into partnership with her father. The extension had been cleverly designed to provide adequate accommodation and working facilities but at the same time to blend in well with the charm of the old house. The waiting-room appeared full, the patients staring at her with interest as she passed and, as she tapped on Grant's door, Alison wondered if she should offer to help with surgery. She wasn't certain, however, how such an offer would be received. He probably wouldn't want to know, she thought grimly as he called out in answer to her knock; he probably wouldn't want her anywhere near his patients.

He glanced up as she opened the door, his surprise at seeing her registering in his eyes, then before she could speak his expression changed and just for a moment there was something there in the slightly narrowed eyes that struck a chord in her memory, something that made her heart beat faster.

She swallowed. 'Sorry to interrupt, but am I right in thinking you've been to the hospital?'

He nodded and rose to his feet and she came right into the room, closing the door behind her, shutting out the growing noise from the waiting-room.

'I came to see what you've found out.'

He frowned, indicating for her to take a seat. 'I don't understand.'

She ignored his offer to sit down and stared at him across the desk. He'd hardly changed at all—in fact he looked exactly the same as when he'd sauntered into her life four years ago and played such havoc. But she mustn't think of that now.

'The post-mortem.' She had difficulty in keeping her voice even. 'Wasn't that why you went to the hospital?'

He stared at her for a long moment then slowly he sat down again and said, 'I went to the hospital to visit a patient who had a colostomy yesterday.'

'OK——' she gave a little dismissive gesture with her hands '—but didn't you ask about the post-mortem while you were there? You told me you would take care of all the arrangements, Grant.' She stared at him.

'That's right, I did.' He took a deep breath then began toying with a stethoscope which lay on the desk before him.

She wondered why he was being so evasive. 'Surely the facts will need to go to the coroner.' She frowned. 'It was, after all, a sudden death.'

'No, Alison,' he said quietly, looking up.

'What do you mean, no? Are you implying that because my father was a doctor the law doesn't apply?'

'I'm not implying anything of the sort.' His tone was quiet, patient. 'The law's the same for everyone.'

'Then what. . .?' Her bewilderment grew.

'What I'm saying is that it wasn't exactly a sudden death.'

She continued staring at him, then suddenly, afraid that her legs wouldn't bear her weight any longer, she sat down heavily. 'What do you mean?' she asked at last, and her voice was barely more than a whisper.

'Your father was suffering from ischemic heart disease.'

'What?' She could hardly believe what she was hearing.

'He'd had several attacks of angina pectoris——'

'But that's impossible. I would have known if he was ill.'

Coolly he raised his eyebrows. 'You haven't been here, Alison.'

She flushed at the implied criticism. 'Maybe not, but I would still have known. . . He would have told me. . .' She glared at Grant then, as another thought struck her, she swept on. 'Besides, if that had been the case he would have been having treatment. . .'

'He was having treatment——'

'As far as I know,' she carried on, interrupting him in mid-sentence, 'he wasn't even registered with a doctor; he'd never been ill. . .' Then she stopped as she realised what he had just said. 'What do you mean, he was having treatment?'

'Exactly that,' he replied quietly. 'Miles had been receiving medical attention for the past year.'

'But who from?' She stared at him in astonishment,

but before he had a chance to answer there came a tap at the door and Sue popped her head round.

'What is it, Sue?' Grant looked up quickly.

'I've brought the records for surgery.'

'Thanks.' He grimaced as he took the extra-large pile of records.

'Are you ready for the first patient yet?' The glance the receptionist threw Alison was apprehensive, as if she knew she was interrupting something crucial.

'Not quite. I won't be long.' He watched as the girl left the room, remaining silent until she closed the door.

'Your father was registered with me, Alison,' he said simply at last.

'You!' She said it as if that had been the last thing she had expected to hear.

'Is that so incredible?' he asked.

'I don't know.' She shook her head in bewilderment. 'I would have thought if he had got round to registering with anyone it might have been Robert Frampton. . . They were friends. . .' She trailed off uncertainly.

'It made much more sense to be registered with me. I was, after all, on the premises,' he replied mildly, but Alison wasn't listening.

'If as you say, he was your patient——' she leaned forward, '—you must have known about his heart disease.'

'Yes, Alison, I did. Of course I did.'

'Did anyone else know?'

'Not that I'm aware of.'

'Why didn't he tell me?' There was pain and bewilderment in her eyes now and she knew he saw it there.

'He chose not to. It was his decision.'

She stared up at him, then suddenly the tension of the last few days reached a peak, something snapped in her head and she stood up.

'So why the hell didn't you tell me?' Furiously she brought her clenched fists down on her father's desk and Grant flinched.

'You know the rules, Alison, as well as I do,' he said quietly.

'You could have warned me!' she cried, ignoring what he had just said. 'You knew I would have wanted to know—knew I would have wanted to say a proper goodbye—and you denied me that!'

'Your father didn't want you to know. It could have gone on for some time and he didn't want it hanging over you, clouding every aspect of your life.'

'Oh, so you discussed me, did you, the two of you?' She glared angrily at him across the desk. 'What else did you come up with?' she demanded. 'What else did you decide would be good for me?'

Grant shook his head but, not giving him the chance to answer, Alison swept on. 'Didn't you stop and consider that it might be good for me to have had the chance to see him again for one last time? Didn't you?'

He didn't answer and for a moment her eyes blazed, then through gritted teeth she said, 'Damn you, Grant! Damn and blast you to hell!'

He remained silent following her outburst, allowing her time to recover, then quietly he said, 'He was my patient, Alison, and I had to respect his confidentiality. He was also my partner and, of late, my friend.'

'And what about me? I was his daughter! Did

you care nothing for me, for my feelings?'

Helplessly she faced him, then with a strangled cry she turned and rushed from the room past a startled Sue and past the waiting patients, all thoughts of helping him gone now, swept aside in her helpless angry grief.

Later that night when her anger had subsided she lay in bed listening to the rustlings and creakings of the house. Once she'd had the chance to calm down, the professional side of her had recognised that Grant had been quite correct in not telling her of her father's condition, but she still felt hurt that she had been excluded from what had been happening at Fairacre. Both Grant and Hilda had implied that she should have visited more often, and deep down she knew they were right.

Restlessly she tossed and turned, sleep eluding her, and in the end she gave up the battle and, slipping out of bed, pulled on her robe and padded to the window.

The garden and the estuary beyond were bathed in soft moonlight. Opening the window, she placed her elbows on the windowsill and breathed in the cool night air.

The reason she'd kept away from Fairacre was quite simple—she hadn't wanted to be anywhere near Grant Ashton, hadn't wanted any reminders of the way things had once been between them. And it didn't take much to remind her. With a deep sigh she rested her chin on her hands.

Even now she could recall the exact moment, four years before, when she had first set eyes on him.

It had been the beginning of her summer vacation from her medical school in London, and she had been lying on a sunbed out there in the garden. . .if she leaned forward she could see the exact spot, bathed in moonlight now. The day had been warm, the air heavy with the scent of roses. . . His feet had made no sound as he'd crossed the grass and she had only been aware of his presence when she'd opened her eyes and found him staring down at her.

Startled, she had tipped back her sunhat and struggled to sit up.

'Sorry—I made you jump.' His voice had been deep, pleasant, the green eyes had held a hint of amusement and the dark hair had flopped forward over his forehead.

'It's OK, but I think you're a little off course. . . The patients' entrance is round there. . .' She'd pointed to the side of the house.

'Oh, I'm not a patient.' The glint of amusement had become even more pronounced as his gaze had taken in her long, tanned legs, then flickered to her hair, tendrils of which had escaped from her hat and were framing her face. 'I'm here to work.'

'To work. . .?' She'd frowned, then realisation had dawned and she'd sat up straight. 'Oh, you must be my father's new partner!'

'None other.' He'd crouched beside her and held out his hand.

From the moment his fingers had touched hers she was lost. . . If only she had known then what would happen, how different things might have been. But she'd had no inkling—how could she? She had loved him almost from that moment and later she could have sworn he loved her.

Her heart twisted as she allowed herself to recall that magical summer: moonlight walks on the beach on nights such as this, barefoot through the surf, sailing trips in the sun with the wind in her hair, kisses that tasted of salt. . .and, later, making love in their own secret place, far from prying eyes, spending every possible moment together until her vacation was over.

'I don't want to go back.' She'd clung to him in the darkness on the night before she was to leave.

'You have to go.' He'd held her tightly but his voice had been husky with emotion. 'You know you do. It's what you've always wanted.'

And he'd been right. For as long as she could remember she'd wanted to be a doctor and she'd worked hard to get to medical school. But she'd never been truly in love before, and now all she wanted in the world was simply to be with him, every moment of every day.

'I'll come home,' she'd whispered, holding him close, 'as often as I can. . .every weekend. . .it won't make any difference to us. . .'

And it hadn't. The months had passed in a haze of yearning, letters, phone calls and endless trips home. And he. . .he'd felt the same way. . .at least—she blinked—she'd thought he had. . .could have sworn he had. . . Oh, how naïve she'd been. . .how young, how vulnerable. . .because when that dreadful day had come and he'd told her he hadn't meant to get serious she'd stared at him in disbelief.

It had been one weekend early the following summer and they had been returning to Fairacre across the fields after walking the causeway. She had been aware that there was something wrong ever since she had arrived home, aware that something was different. Grant had seemed cool, distant, and her unease had grown steadily. Nothing, however, had really prepared her for the moment of truth.

'What do you mean, not get serious?'

'Exactly that.' He'd looked uncomfortable.

'But I thought it was serious. It was for me, Grant. I thought it was for you.' Her bewilderment had been only too apparent and he'd turned away from her as if unable to face the pain in her eyes.

'I'm sorry, Alison. . .but I think we should cool it.'

'Is there someone else?' she'd demanded.

He'd shaken his head. 'No. I'm just not ready for this type of relationship and I don't think you are either.'

She'd been angry then. 'How dare you tell me what I'm ready for?'

'I'm sorry,' he'd said again. 'I'd hoped we could still be friends.'

'Friends!' Her disbelief complete, she'd walked away from him then, back through the path across the fields.

Later they had quarrelled, quarrelled bitterly, before she had returned to London. But it had hurt. Oh, how it had hurt.

She had done her best to rebuild her life, had worked hard at her studies and at first had kept herself to herself. Later she had made friends, had even tried a few relationships. One, with a fellow student, Simon, had at first seemed promising, but like the others it had fizzled out...

She had avoided seeing Grant since and had thought she might be over it after all this time...but coming home to Fairacre had only stirred the memories of the way it had been...and it still hurt.

Suddenly she was angry again, angry that he still had the power to move her. Stepping back, she closed the window with a bang.

After the funeral she would go, get away from Fairacre, from the painful memories of her father, but most of all she would get away from Grant Ashton and the memories of what had happened between them.

The day of the funeral dawned fresh and clear, the slight early morning mist quickly giving way to bright April sunshine, and it seemed to Alison that the entire population of the small town had turned out to pay their last respects to her father. They crowded into the Norman church on the green, filling the pews and aisles, the sombre blacks and greys of their clothes in sharp contrast to the masses of spring flowers that still filled the church from the previous week's Easter celebration.

Alison was touched to see the extent of the town's regard for her father, but she herself viewed the proceedings as if from a distance. It all seemed unreal and she found it hard to believe it was actually happening. Her father had few family living—a cousin who had travelled from Yorkshire and two nephews and a niece whom Alison could barely remember. Throughout the day she was conscious of Grant Ashton's presence as he automatically seemed to take charge.

Hilda had prepared refreshments for family and close friends but, even in the familiar surroundings of Fairacre, Alison felt stiff and unnatural, as if she was functioning in some terrible dream, her responses to condolences stilted and false. She longed for everyone to go so that she could be alone. Her head ached with the tension of unshed tears and she yearned for the oblivion of sleep, but there were farewells to be made.

'Goodbye; thank you for coming.'

'He was a good man, the doctor.'

'Yes, goodbye.'

'Your father will be sadly missed in Woodbridge.'

'Thank you for coming. Goodbye.'

'It's been a sad day, Alison.'

This voice in the midst of the murmured pleasantries was instantly recognisable and she looked up quickly. Godfrey Warner, a partner in the firm of her father's solicitors, and his close friend, stood in front of her.

'Yes, Godfrey, it has.' She'd known Godfrey all her life and knew he meant what he was saying.

He hesitated as if he wanted to say more, then, glancing over his shoulder, he said, 'Will you call into chambers tomorrow morning, Alison? We need to discuss your father's will.'

'Yes, all right.'

'I've asked Grant Ashton to come,' Godfrey added.

They both turned spontaneously and looked towards

the large sashcord windows where Grant stood in conversation with a consultant from the local hospital. As if he sensed their scrutiny he looked up and his gaze met Alison's. In spite of her anguish of the night before, Alison had been grateful for his support and had been content to lean on him. Now she was aware of something else in his look, something she wasn't immediately able to define.

It was the sound of Godfrey Warner clearing his throat, as if he had suddenly become aware of an undercurrent, that made her look away and when, a little later, she returned from showing Godfrey to the front door Grant was no longer in the room.

By that time the house was empty of mourners and was quiet, apart from the faint clatter of dishes from the kitchen where Hilda and her friend Doris were washing up.

With a deep sigh Alison took off the hat she'd worn to church, upinned her hair and shook it free, catching sight of herself in the mirror over the mantelpiece as she did so. She was faintly shocked by her appearance; her face looked white and drawn, her dark eyes huge, the purple smudges beneath them evidence of her recent lack of sleep.

With a hopeless little gesture she turned from the mirror and wandered aimlessly to the window, where she stood for a long time simply staring at the garden, the neatly tended flowerbeds and the immaculate lawns that ran down to a little coppice at the very edge of the estuary.

She had loved this place so much. It had been the

place of her childhood, the place of adventure, of happiness, a place of friendships, girlish dreams, first love. . .

Angrily she turned away. That was all gone now; even her beloved father had gone, and there was nothing left, nothing here for her now at Fairacre.

At a slight sound from the doorway she looked round sharply. Grant was standing there watching her. How long he'd been there she had no idea. Had he seen her take off her hat, shake out her hair? Had he watched her as she'd scrutinised her appearance? Read her thoughts as she'd stared at the garden, recalling the past? She had no way of knowing, but even the possibility irritated her.

'I didn't know you were there.' It came out more sharply than she had intended, then, seeing the surprise in his eyes at her brusqueness, she was immediately contrite. He had, after all, been her support during the last few days. But that was over now. Life had to go on.

'Did you want something, Grant?' Her tone was softer.

'I just wondered if you were all right. Today has been a great strain.'

She gave a helpless shrug. 'Yes, it has,' she agreed. 'But I'm coping. . .'

'Fancy a walk?' He nodded towards the window.

She hesitated. She shouldn't. She knew that.

He seemed to misinterpret the reason for her hesitation. 'I have a while before surgery.'

'All right—but let me change first. I feel like someone else in this black.'

'Me too.' He smiled and she felt her heart twist. It was the first time since she'd come home that she'd seen his features relax.

CHAPTER TWO

IT WAS cool in the softness of the spring evening and Alison was glad of the thick sweater she wore over her leggings. They crossed the lawn in silence, their feet making no sound on the thick emerald carpet.

'I owe you an apology,' she said awkwardly at last.

'What for?' He frowned.

'Yesterday, I accused you of keeping my father's condition from me. It was wrong of me. I'm sorry.'

'It was understandable that you felt the way you did. I would probably have felt the same way in your shoes.'

'Even so, it wasn't your fault.'

They walked on, then Grant threw her a sidelong glance. 'I was wondering,' he said at last, 'what your plans are.'

'My plans?' She half turned towards him. 'What do you mean?'

He thrust his hands into the pockets of his jeans, hunching his shoulders inside the navy fisherman's sweater he wore. 'I wondered what you intend doing now that your training is complete.'

'I shall be going back to Suffolk. I'm hoping they'll keep me on.'

'As a partner?' He raised his eyebrows.

'Not immediately. But perhaps soon.'

They fell silent again, the stillness of the coppice all around them, acid green buds bursting on new elm saplings, velvet pussy willow and trembling yellow catkins.

'So you're happy, then, in Suffolk?'

She shot him a glance but he was staring straight ahead, chewing the stem of a blade of grass he had plucked from the bank.

'I've made a life for myself,' she answered carefully, then, before he could probe further, went on quickly, 'I like the town, I've got to know the people and I've made...friends...lots of friends...'

'Ah, yes, friends,' he murmured.

While they had been talking they had reached the far edge of the coppice and the footpath that led across the fields to the estuary, and automatically they both stopped. In the past when they had taken that very walk they had ended up at the marina aboard her father's boat.

Grant looked at her enquiringly. There was no need for words. He too remembered.

She shook her head and turned back towards the house. It was too dangerous. It had all happened on evenings such as this. Not spring, high summer, but the air had been just as heady, just as seductive, and the man at her side had been the same.

She was still fighting nostalgia, battling with a sense of what might have been, when they reached the house, while Grant was once again silent and straight-faced.

Already patients were arriving for evening surgery and Hilda met them in the hallway.

'There's an emergency call for you, Dr Ashton,' she said, handing him a slip of paper.

'It's the far side of Freshwater,' he said after studying

the message Hilda had taken. 'I may be a long time. Gill hasn't arrived yet—could you tell the patients, please, Hilda?'

'Of course, Dr Ashton.' Hilda began unbuttoning the overall she was wearing to protect the navy blue dress she'd worn to the funeral.

Grant glanced at Alison and for the first time she saw the fatigue in his eyes; as he turned away and began walking to his consulting-room, she called him back.

'Wait a minute, Grant.'

'What is it?' He turned.

She swallowed. 'Would you like me to start surgery for you?'

'You?' He stared at her and something in the look caused her to flush.

'Yes, me. Why not?' She was aware of Hilda's expression—one of anticipation. 'I'm fully qualified.'

'I know that. . .'

'And perfectly capable.'

'I don't doubt that. . .'

'Then what. . .?' She frowned.

'It's just that we thought you'd never ask, didn't we, Hilda?'

With a tight little smile he was gone, leaving her staring after him. When she turned to Hilda she was in time to see a smile on the housekeeper's face before she too disappeared back down the passage to the kitchen.

Moments later she heard Grant's car start up, and slowly she crossed Reception to make her way to his consulting-room.

As she passed her father's room she stopped and on a sudden impulse pushed open the door and stood for a moment on the threshold.

The room was achingly familiar—the large oak desk beneath high rounded windows, the leather couch in one corner, glass-fronted cabinets full of books, and the various items of medical equipment lying just where her father had left them when he'd finished his last surgery moments before his heart attack. Slowly she walked right into the room, shutting the door behind her.

The very essence of her father was here in this room —the smell of the sandalwood soap he'd used, the whiff of the cigars he'd occasionally smoked, and another, more elusive smell—the tang of the sea which he had so loved.

She reached the desk, stared down at the blotter and at a notepad that lay open on the polished surface. Moving the pad towards her, she caught sight of his small, almost illegible handwriting and, feeling her throat constrict, she turned sharply away but, as she did so, on the back of the door she saw his jacket, the old navy blue one he used to wear for sailing.

Crossing to the door again, she stood looking at the jacket, then, with a choked cry, buried her face in its folds and allowed her hot tears to dampen the fabric.

She didn't know how long she stood there as the grief she had kept tightly controlled finally flowed, and in the end it was the growing noise from the waiting-room that reminded her she had a job to do. Walking swiftly to the washbasin, she splashed her face with cold water, and was just wondering if she had time to go upstairs and apply some make-up when the door slowly opened and Gill's face appeared.

'Oh, it's you, Alison,' she said. 'I heard a noise in here and I wondered who on earth it was.'

'Yes, Gill, it's only me.' She managed a smile, knowing the secretary had seen her red eyes and must have guessed she had been crying. There was a moment's silence as they looked around the room then Alison said, 'I've agreed to start surgery for Dr Ashton; he's been called out.'

'That's kind—I'll get the records for you.' Gill paused, one hand on the door-handle, and threw her a curious glance. 'Did you mean in here?'

Alison looked round again. 'No, Gill, not in here. I'll go to Dr Ashton's room.'

Gill nodded. She looked relieved, as if it would somehow be beyond her to explain the situation to the patients—that it was Dr Alison Kennedy sitting at Dr Miles Kennedy's desk.

Shutting the door firmly behind her, Alison followed Gill to Reception where she collected the patient's records then took them to Grant's consulting-room.

The room was bright with the last of the afternoon sun and a vase of daffodils added a splash of colour to the windowsill. Several prints from the French Impressionist school dotted the walls and a selection of children's paintings and drawings was pinned to a cork board behind the door. A computer stood on the desk and several brightly coloured containers filled with toys were tucked beneath the examination couch.

Alison looked round in surprise; she hadn't expected such touches from Grant, but then, she thought, she knew very little about how he operated as a doctor.

Slowly she sat down at his desk and began looking through the patients' records. Moments later Gill came through on the intercom and asked if she was ready for the first patient.

'Yes, Gill,' Alison replied. 'I see it's Seth Attrill—you'd better send him in.'

Seconds later the door opened and an elderly man with a weatherbeaten complexion stood on the threshold surveying her from beneath jutting grey eyebrows.

'Well, I'll be darned!' Removing his cap, he scratched his head and added, 'If it isn't Miss Alison. Now if that's not a sight for sore eyes, I don't know what is!'

In spite of herself Alison felt a smile touch her lips. Seth Attrill was something of a local character—for many years he'd been greatly in demand as a gardener and one of his many jobs had been to tend the gardens at Fairacre. Alison knew he'd retired recently and lived with his wife, Mabel, in one of the modern flats that had been built near the marina.

'Hello, Seth,' she said, then, indicating a chair, she added, 'Come in and sit down.'

'Terrible turnout about your poor dad.' Seth, still dressed in the Sunday-best tweeds he'd worn to church, stood in the middle of the room shaking his head. 'Terrible. We can't hardly believe it—none of us. Why, I was only talking to him last Wednesday; he'd been to see my great-niece—just had a little 'un, she has—and I met him on the way out—he seemed fine then. . .'

'Yes, Seth, he was; it was very sudden,' replied Alison, as she began to realise that this surgery could be far from easy.

'Y'know, him being a doctor and all that, you'd have thought he'd have known something, wouldn't you? I said as much to old Jim Stevens when we paid our respects this afternoon. Jim reckons he was so busy looking after everyone else, he never had no time to doctor himself.'

'Quite.' While Seth was talking Alison quickly scanned his records, then looked up. 'Now, Seth, please sit down and tell me what seems to be the trouble.'

'Eh?' He stared at her through watery blue eyes, then turned his head to look at the chair she was indicating. 'Oh, yes, right.' He sat down heavily but still appeared reluctant to get on to the reason for his visit. 'So have you taken over now, then, Miss Alison?' he asked curiously.

'Only for tonight, Seth,' she replied firmly. 'I'm simply helping Dr Ashton out, that's all.'

'Oh, I see. Nice young fellow, Dr Ashton—not Dr Kennedy, of course, but pleasant enough in his own way. . .I was only saying yesterday——'

'Seth! Please can we get to the point? I have a lot of patients to see.'

'What? Oh, yes, yes, right you are.' He paused, stared at her for a long moment, shifted uncomfortably on his chair then stood up again.

'I think maybe I'd better come back when Dr Ashton's here,' he muttered.

'Seth, please sit down and tell me what's troubling

you.' Alison struggled to keep the exasperation from her voice.

'It don't seem right somehow, you a young woman. . . Why, I remember you when you were in your pram. . .and now. . .' He trailed off in embarrassment.

'Seth,' she said gently, 'I may well be the same girl you remember as a baby but I am also a qualified doctor and I won't be shocked by anything you might tell me or show me—now, let me guess, is it your hernia playing you up again?'

He stared at her in astonishment. 'How in the world did you know that?'

'I did my homework.'

'Your homework?' He scratched his head in bewilderment.

'Yes.' She held up his medical notes. 'Gill gave me these before I started surgery. So let's get on, shall we? If you would like to slip off your trousers and lie on the bench.'

As Seth slunk away behind the screen to undress, Alison suppressed a smile.

Steadily she worked through the list of patients but it proved a slow process. Like Seth, most of them— apart from the newcomers to Woodbridge, who eyed her with some suspicion—knew her and wanted to offer their condolences. She was just beginning to wonder whether Grant was ever going to return when the door opened and a tall, blonde-haired woman strolled into the room.

Alison's heart sank. She glanced at the notes in front of her and saw that the woman's surname, Masterton, had been crossed out and Rossi inserted. 'I didn't realise it was you, Cheryl,' she said. 'You've changed your name.

The woman laughed. 'Rossi is my married name.' She sat down, crossing long, slim legs.

'So what can I do for you?' Alison had known Cheryl since they had both attended the same girls' school on the east side of the island. She hadn't liked her much even then.

'I've run out of my pills.'

'I see—I gather you were my father's patient, not Dr Ashton's?'

'Oh, no, I'm not Dr Ashton's patient.' She arched finely drawn eyebrows. 'But what difference does that make?'

'No difference.' Alison shook her head. 'It's just that I understood my father held a Well Woman clinic. I simply wondered why you hadn't attended that for a pill check.'

'I told you—I ran out. Besides, it isn't all of us who can get to afternoon clinics—some of us have work to do.'

Alison swallowed. 'Quite. What do you do these days, Cheryl?'

'I work for Ken Bridges at the marina.'

'I see.' She stood up. 'Right, let's just take your blood-pressure, shall we?'

'Whatever for?' Cheryl stared up at her in apparent amazement. 'I only want a packet of pills, for God's sake.'

'And I only want to check your blood-pressure,' replied Alison calmly. 'You're not my patient, Cheryl, and I don't intend to prescribe anything for you without checking first.'

'But I always have these pills—I just happen to have run out, that's all.' She glared at her, and Alison sat down again and began replacing the cap on her pen.

For a long moment there was silence, then Cheryl gave an exaggerated sigh. 'Oh, very well, suit yourself.' She slipped off her jacket and rolled up the sleeve of her silk blouse.

Without a word Alison stood up, moved round the desk, and set up the sphygmomanometer. When she had satisfied herself that Cheryl's blood-pressure was normal and ignoring the 'I told you so' expression on the other woman's face, she wrote out the prescription for the particular brand of contraceptive pill previously prescribed by her father.

'So what's going to happen here now?' asked Cheryl as she replaced her jacket and took the prescription form from Alison.

'What do you mean, what's going to happen?'

'Will you always be taking Dr Kennedy's surgeries?' The expression on Cheryl's face, clearly indicating that she hoped that wasn't to be the case, goaded Alison into being evasive.

'Nothing's been decided yet,' she replied shortly.

'I understood you have your own practice—don't you have to get back?'

Alison stood up and pressed the buzzer for the next patient. 'No, I don't yet have my own practice.'

'Oh?' Cheryl frowned. 'I was told you worked somewhere in Suffolk.'

'I have just completed my GP training at a group

practice in Suffolk, certainly.' Suddenly Alison felt annoyed that she had felt compelled to answer Cheryl's questions, and found herself wondering how the other girl seemed to know so much about her. 'Now, if you'll excuse me, I must get on,' she added firmly.

With a shrug Cheryl left the room, and Alison realised that she had been the only patient that evening who hadn't offered sympathy on her father's death.

She'd seen three more patients—a child with tonsillitis, an elderly lady with phlebitis and a young man with a throat virus—before Grant finally returned from the emergency call.

'Sorry to have been so long,' he said from the open doorway. 'Any problems?' he added, not giving her a chance to speak.

She shook her head. 'None at all. Were you expecting there to have been?'

'No. Why should I? You're a doctor, after all.'

Something in his manner made her flinch and she stood up. 'Now that you're here, you might as well take over. Most of the patients I saw were my father's —I'm afraid yours are still waiting, but I thought it might be easier that way.'

'What were the patients' reactions to finding you here?' He suddenly sounded curious.

'Some of them couldn't believe the child they saw grow up is actually now a doctor.' She gave a tight little smile. 'Others thought I'd simply stepped into my father's shoes.'

'And what was your reaction to that?'

'I soon put them straight,' she said firmly, ignoring

the quizzical expression on his face. 'I told them I'd be returning to Suffolk just as soon as things have been sorted out.'

CHAPTER THREE

IT WAS raining the following morning, heavy April showers interspersed by quick bursts of sunshine and accompanied by a fresh sea breeze. Alison and Grant walked the short distance to the chambers of Warner, Rolf and Son, a pleasant Georgian house overlooking the square, and were shown straight into Godfrey Warner's office.

'Alison, my dear.' Godfrey rose to greet them and Alison was forced to swallow an unexpected lump that rose in her throat, for something about Godfrey had suddenly reminded her of her father. The two men had been friends for many years; they had been members of the same sailing club and had played golf together.

Moving round to the front of the desk, Godfrey kissed her cheek then shook hands with Grant, at the same time indicating for them both to sit down.

After the usual pleasantries, coffee served by Godfrey's secretary and a few necessary preliminaries, Godfrey got down to the reason for their visit.

'Miles appointed me as executor of his will which was drawn up by my partner, Sam Rolf,' he said. 'It's quite straightforward, as you will see.'

He went on to mention a few personal bequests, including a small legacy for Hilda Lloyd, before moving on to the disposal of the remainder of the estate.

Miles Kennedy's quite considerable assets by way of savings, investments, shares and bonds had all been left to his beloved daughter, Alison Kennedy, to dispose of in whatever way she chose.

Alison's eyes misted over and Godfrey glanced up.

'We now come to the partnership and to the house, Fairacre,' he said, 'and for this purpose I think I had better read Miles's wishes to you very carefully so that there can be no confusion or misunderstanding.' He cleared his throat, rustled his papers and began reading again.

Alison, watching him, had a sudden premonition, a sense of warning, but nothing could really have prepared her for what she was about to hear.

'"One of the greatest joys of my life,"' Godfrey read, '"was when my daughter, Alison, decided to follow me into the medical profession, in so doing maintaining a family tradition passed down to me from my father and his father before him."'

Godfrey glanced up, smiled, and said, 'We come now, Alison, to your father's property and business interests. He continued reading. '"Four years ago, I was persuaded, against my better judgement, to take a partner. Until that time I had successfully maintained a single-man practice and I saw no reason for change. Fate, alas, decreed otherwise in terms of increased population, and I was forced to seek assistance. Grant Ashton came recommended by a colleague and our partnership was established. My house, Fairacre, was converted to provide adequate space for two surgeries and accommodation for my partner, who subsequently became a shareholder in the property. It is now my wish that my share of the same property passes to my daughter Alison.'"

Godfrey glanced at her again and Alison nodded. It was what she had expected. She stirred in her seat, thinking Godfrey had finished, but to her surprise he continued reading.

'"The early days of partnership weren't without their stormy moments, as I'm sure Grant himself will testify, but we persevered and we developed, I believe, a good, solid working relationship from which I hope the residents of Woodbridge have consequently benefited.

"I should like to feel that this sense of continuity will continue after my death and to this objective it is my last and dearest wish that my daughter Alison should take over my share of the practice, that she and Grant Ashton be partners, that the house, Fairacre, shall continue to provide adequate premises for the partnership, and that they will continue to serve the people of Woodbridge to the best of their abilities."'

As Godfrey Warner finished speaking, Alison stared at him in stunned silence.

'Are you all right, Alison?' he asked quietly at last.

Gradually she became aware of Godfrey's concerned expression, but her mind was racing. There had been some mistake. Her father would never have expected her to go into partnership with Grant; he knew they hadn't got on. She had guessed he would leave his share of Fairacre to her and she had already thought that Grant would want to continue practising there. She'd even gone so far as to think that she would lease her share of the property to him so that he could bring in another partner. Surely she could do that, then go back to Suffolk, to the life she had made for herself, to Diana Richards and the practice, to her friends. . .

At a slight movement beside her she turned sharply and found Grant himself looking every bit as stricken as she felt.

'Did you know about this?' she demanded, ignoring Godfrey Warner's ineffectual attempt to intervene.

Grant shook his head. 'No. Nothing.'

'I don't believe you,' she said flatly.

'Alison, please——' Godfrey began, half rising out of his chair, but Alison carried on sharply.

'He knew my father had a serious heart condition but chose not to tell me—there's a very good chance he knew about this as well.'

Even as she spoke she could hear the trace of hysteria in her voice. The situation was impossible. . . ludicrous even.

'That's rubbish, Alison—you're overwrought.' Grant stood up and, looking down at her, said, 'I knew nothing of this, and if I had I assure you I would have had something to say about it.'

'But is it so terrible?' Godfrey, in an attempt to avert what now seemed to be becoming a full-scale row in his chambers, leaned back in his chair and looked from one to the other of them.

Alison gazed back incredulously and Godfrey gave a helpless little shrug.

'Is there a way round this?' asked Grant suddenly.

Godfrey stared at them both for a long moment then, leaning forward, placed his elbows on the desk, making a temple of his hands.

'There could,' he said at last, choosing his words with obvious care, 'certainly legally be a way round this.' He paused. 'Alison, you could, in theory, sell or even lease your half of the house to Grant, and he could take another partner. Alternatively, the property could be sold and the proceeds split. . .or, I suppose, Alison, you could buy Grant out.'

Alison gave a sigh of relief, but Godfrey hadn't finished.

'However,' he went on, 'I don't quite understand what the problem is. To me it sounds an ideal situation.'

'The problem, Godfrey,' said Alison firmly, 'is that there is absolutely no way that Dr Ashton and myself could work together, let alone form a partnership.'

'I'll endorse that,' said Grant tightly, then, before Godfrey had chance to comment further, he went on, 'You said, Godfrey, that legally there was a way round this. But you seem to have other doubts.'

'As I said,' Godfrey replied evenly, 'legally the situation can be resolved, as can most affairs of this nature. . .morally, however, it's an entirely different matter.'

'What do you mean?' Alison looked up swiftly, and sensed rather than saw Grant's similar response.

'We are talking here,' said Godfrey, looking pointedly at each of them in turn, 'of the dying wish of your father, Alison, and your partner, Grant.'

There was a moment's silence before Godfrey continued. 'It was a dream Miles had had for some time to be able to pass the practice over to the two of you —to know,' he added, 'that you would both carry it on in the same tradition as he and his father had before him.'

The only sound that could be heard in the room was the swish of tyres outside on the wet road.

When Alison and Grant both remained silent Godfrey spoke again.

'Neither of you knows this,' he said quietly, 'but before Miles knew of his illness he had made plans to retire.'

Alison looked up sharply and saw her surprise reflected on Grant's features.

'But,' Godfrey went on, 'he had the same partnership plans for the practice involving the two of you. It meant a great deal to him and it would be very wrong of you both to dismiss his wishes lightly.'

He paused to allow time for his words to sink in, then finally he said, 'I can see at this moment that you both think this arrangement would have no chance of success,' He paused, then said, 'I wonder, could I make a suggestion?'

Alison glanced at Grant. His expression was shuttered and she wondered what he was thinking. He was probably even more horrified than she was at her father's wishes. Before she had the chance to speak, however, Grant answered Godfrey's question.

'What's your suggestion, Godfrey?'

Godfrey hesitated. 'Why not a trial partnership?' he said at last. 'Say for six months. At the end of that time, surely, you would know whether or not it was going to work.'

'Look,' he added when they both remained silent, 'go away now, think about it, then get back to me, and if you decide to go ahead I'll draw up the necessary agreement to cover the trial period.'

For a long moment Alison stared at the solicitor, then she rose to her feet and with a muttered apology she hurried from the room, into the hall then out into the square.

It was still raining and she paused for one moment to put up her umbrella. Grant caught her up a few moments later. He'd turned up the collar of his black trench coat and his shoulders were hunched against the rain.

They walked the short distance to Fairacre in tight-lipped silence. As they turned in at the drive it was Alison who broke it.

'It would never work,' she said abruptly.

'No, of course not,' he replied.

'It's out of the question.'

'Absolutely.'

'I can't imagine what my father was thinking of.' She gave a sharp little gesture with her free hand. 'He knew the situation between us. I can only imagine he must have taken leave of his senses.'

'So where do we go from here?' He threw her a sidelong glance.

'I shall be returning to Suffolk just as soon as I can.'

'And Fairacre? The practice?'

By this time they had almost reached the house and spontaneously they slowed and looked up at the building.

Alison shrugged. 'Something will have to be worked out—as Godfrey said, you could always buy me out

—that would be the most sensible option in the circumstances.'

'I thought you would want to stay here,' he said tightly.

'Whatever gave you that idea?' She turned slightly, raising her eyebrows.

He didn't answer immediately and suddenly she became very aware of him, his nearness, and she felt herself stiffen in defence.

'There are many reasons,' he said quietly. 'Fairacre is your home...there are memories...'

'Some are memories I would far rather forget,' she answered sharply, then, putting her head down, she hurried into the house, leaving Grant to follow.

Alison walked again that afternoon after the rain had stopped, only this time she walked alone, through the coppice and along the bank of the estuary. Grant was out on house calls and she hadn't seen him since their return from the solicitor. In spite of having made her decision to return to Suffolk, her thoughts inevitably turned to her father and his wishes. Godfrey had urged both her and Grant to think hard about what her father had wanted, and if she was honest there was a part of her that would have liked nothing better than to return to the island, to her beloved Fairacre, and to take over her father's share in the practice he had worked so hard to build. It was certainly a practical solution and, for her, a wonderful professional opportunity, one that shouldn't be dismissed lightly.

Maybe, she thought as she tramped through the wet, coarse grass, she should reconsider. But how could she? She gave a deep sigh and pushed her hands deeply into the pockets of her waxed jacket. Even if she accepted the situation there was no way that Grant would. He had made that quite plain. He obviously didn't want her there. On the other hand she had as much right to be there as he did—more in fact. Perhaps —she gave a grim little smile—perhaps he should be the one to go. Maybe she should buy him out and bring in a new partner—but that, she knew, would be crazy from a professional and practical point of view. The patients had already lost one half of the partnership they had come to trust and respect; it wouldn't do for them to lose the other half.

No, the only option was the one she had already decided on; she would return to Suffolk and hope it wouldn't be too long before she had some sort of career opportunity. She had to get away from Grant. Her heart twisted at the thought—it had disturbed her seeing him again, disturbed her much more than she cared to admit and the only answer now was to put as much distance between them as she possibly could.

She retraced her steps back through the coppice and was crossing the lawn to the house when she looked up and saw that Grant was standing at the French doors watching her. When he realised she had seen him he opened the doors and walked to meet her.

He looked serious, pensive even, and she scanned his features, wondering what had happened to make him look that way.

'Grant?' She stopped and flicked back her hair. 'Is there anything wrong?'

'No.' He too stopped and stared down at her. 'No,

there's nothing wrong. I've just been thinking, that's all.'

'Me too,' she admitted.

'I wonder,' he continued, 'if we haven't been too hasty.' She remained silent and he went on. 'In fact I think we should reconsider.'

'You do?' She raised her eyebrows.

'Yes. I think that Godfrey was quite right and that we shouldn't dismiss your father's last wish so lightly.'

She nodded. 'I've been thinking much the same,' she admitted.

'I feel,' he went on, 'that Warner had a point when he said it was something that was obviously dear to your father's heart. I think we should give it a try.'

Slowly she breathed out. 'You mean——?'

'What Godfrey suggested,' he interrupted. 'A six-month trial—then reconsider the position.'

Her heart thumped and she remained silent for a moment, her mind racing ahead. It was almost as if some telepathy had been at work between them that afternoon and he had been reading her thoughts.

'Well, Alison?' he asked at last. 'Shall we give it a try?'

Still she hesitated, torn between desperately wanting to agree and terrified at putting herself into another vulnerable position.

She took a deep breath. 'Yes, all right, Grant. A six-month trial.' She paused, then added, 'Oh one condition.'

He stared down at her and she found it impossible to read the expression in his eyes.

'Which is?' he said at last.

'That our relationship is strictly professional,' she replied firmly.

He raised his eyebrows. 'But of course,' he said softly, then added, 'What else would it be?'

CHAPTER FOUR

Two weeks later Grant was again at Yarmouth to meet her and they eyed each other warily as she stepped out of the terminal.

'This is getting to be a habit,' she commented as he stowed her luggage in the boot of his BMW. 'I'll have to get myself a car.'

'Your father's Rover is still in the garage,' he said as he took his place beside her. 'There's no reason why you shouldn't use that.'

They were silent as he drove away from the ferry terminal, then as he took the coast road for Woodbridge he threw her a sidelong glance. 'Did you have any problems with your employers?'

She shook her head. 'No, I simply worked my notice. They seemed pleased that I've got such an opportunity and they even went so far as to say they'd consider taking me back if things don't work out.'

'And you? How do you feel?'

'I think you'd better ask me that again in six months' time,' she said wryly, somehow refraining from adding that she still had reservations over the reality of her and Grant's working together.

As if he could read her thoughts he suddenly said, 'I know this isn't an ideal situation, Alison, just as I realise there could be problems, so I think we need to lay down a few ground rules right from the start if we're to get on.'

'What do you mean?' She threw him a startled glance. He was staring straight ahead, apparently concentrating on the winding country road.

'Well, from a working point of view, there shouldn't be too many difficulties,' he answered at last. 'I suggest you take over your father's list of patients and we'll share the on-call in the same way that he and I did.'

'That sounds reasonable.'

'Living arrangements, however, could be a little more difficult.'

'Why?' She frowned. 'I imagine Hilda is still prepared to live in?'

'She is,' he agreed. 'But it was her I was thinking of.'

'I don't understand.'

'When we discussed the situation you made it quite plain that our relationship was to be a professional one.'

'Yes, but I don't see why that should affect Hilda.'

'As you know, Hilda used to prepare meals for your father and myself and we used to eat together.' He paused and Alison wondered what he was going to say. 'I think,' he went on at last, 'to assist Hilda, we should stick to those arrangements. If we start eating separately and at different times it will only make her job more difficult.'

'Of course. . .when I said a professional relationship I didn't mean for us to go to extremes. . .' She felt her cheeks redden.

'Didn't you? I thought that was exactly what you meant,' he said coolly. 'But you needn't worry; if it's a professional relationship you want, then that's what you shall have.'

'Good, that's fine by me,' she snapped.

They drew into the drive at Fairacre and suddenly she felt irritated, goaded by his manner, but as she stepped from the car Hilda appeared on the doorstep to greet her.

'Alison, love, it's good to have you back,' she said simply.

'Hello, Hilda.' Alison almost forgot herself and said it was good to be back—it wouldn't do to say that in front of Grant. But as she accompanied Hilda upstairs to her room and Grant followed more slowly with her luggage she realised that, in spite of all that had happened, it was indeed good to be back.

Hilda had placed freshly cut flowers—narcissus and pink tulips from the garden—in a vase on the dressing-table, while on the windowsill a bowl of fragrant pot-pourri stood beside a framed photograph of Miles Kennedy.

Alison blinked and busied herself with taking off her coat while Grant set her cases down in the middle of the floor then, with a curt nod, strode from the room.

Hilda shut the window, rearranged the curtains, then turned and smiled at Alison. 'It really is good to have you here—the place just hasn't been the same. . .'

'Oh, Hilda!' Alison gulped and, as the older woman opened her arms, she stepped forward to be hugged. 'It is good to be home.'

For a quiet moment they remembered, then Alison moved away and briskly began hauling one of her cases on to the bed while Hilda took out her handkerchief, wiped her eyes, then moved to the door where she paused, one hand on the doorknob.

'Dinner after evening surgery as usual?' she asked, and Alison thought she detected a trace of anxiety in her tone as if she too feared that Alison would want to make changes to the domestic routine.

'Oh, yes, Hilda, thank you,' she said quickly.

'I've done your favourite—steak and kidney pie,' Hilda smiled in relief and Alison didn't have the heart to tell her that these days she ate very little red meat.

'It must be a tremendous relief for Dr Ashton,' said Hilda. 'I really don't know how the poor man has coped. But that'll all change now that you're here to help.'

'That remains to be seen.' Alison pulled a face.

'I can't understand why you two don't get on any more.' Hilda's forehead creased in a frown. 'Why, at one time I even thought——'

'That was a long time ago, Hilda,' Alison interrupted crisply. 'A lot of water's flowed under the bridge since then.'

'He's such a nice man, though, Dr Ashton...his patients adore him...'

'Good for them.' Alison gave a short laugh. 'Now, Hilda, I must shower and change if you want me ready for that steak and kidney pie!'

'I assume you'll be using your father's consulting-room?' Grant helped himself to more creamed parsnips and glanced across the table at Alison.

'Of course.' She nodded, then added, 'Initially I had

reservations but the only other room I could use would be the sitting-room and it seems sensible to use a room that is already equipped.'

'When would you be prepared to start?'

'How about tomorrow?' she asked, then, seeing his raised eyebrows, she said, 'I thought the sooner the better.'

'I agree. I suppose I hadn't assumed you would be ready so soon.'

'Why shouldn't I be?'

He shrugged and poured himself a glass of water. 'I simply thought you might have other things to do, that you might need a little time to sort yourself out.'

'Grant, I'm here for one reason and one reason only; let's not pretend otherwise,' she said stiffly. As she pushed her plate away she heard the telephone ringing and saw Grant lift his head to listen. The ringing stopped and she guessed Hilda had answered it.

'I wasn't aware that there was any pretence,' he said stiffly. 'I shall be more than happy to shift half the workload in your direction and I should the think the patients would be relieved at not having to wait so long to see a doctor——' He broke off as Hilda tapped at the dining-room door then pushed it open. 'What is it, Hilda?' He glanced up.

'An emergency, Dr Ashton—Bert Keenor is having difficulty with his breathing again. His wife is on the phone.'

'I'll speak to her.' He pushed his chair back and stood up. 'Some things never change.' He gave Alison a wry smile and followed Hilda from the room.

He's right there, she thought as the door closed

behind them. Bert Keenor had suffered from chronic obstructive airways disease for as long as she could remember...some things really didn't seem to change...but other things changed out of all recognition.

And that night as she lay in her own bed in her old room and listened to the once familiar creakings of the house and heard Grant come up the stairs and go into his room she realised fully just how much everything had changed.

An hour later she was still awake and wondering if he was asleep or if he too was lying staring into the darkness and thinking. Thinking of how it had once been between them—how wonderful it had once been. Or had it only been wonderful for her? Restlessly she turned on to her side. It wouldn't do to start going over all that again. If she did, she would be sure to have a sleepless night just as she'd had so often in the past when she had allowed herself to agonise over Grant Ashton.

The last thing she wanted was a sleepless night. Word would have got round in Woodbridge that she was taking her father's place and she could be sure of a full surgery, if only with patients suffering from acute curiosity. And besides, she didn't want Grant Ashton thinking she might be suffering from insomnia—he might jump to the wrong conclusions and think that her sleeplessness was due to him.

The harder she tried, however, the more sleep eluded her and when eventually she drifted off it seemed as if her alarm clock awoke her almost immediately. For a few moments she lay listening to the rooster from a nearby farm then, with a sigh, she dragged herself from her bed.

When she took her place at the breakfast-table she felt exhausted and unrefreshed and to her relief there was no sign of Grant.

'He's been called out to a threatened miscarriage,' explained Hilda as she appeared with fresh coffee and toast. 'It's that little Mrs Cotton down at Dubbers Farm—her poor husband sounded frantic on the phone. If she loses this one, it'll be the third.'

'Her third miscarriage?' Alison frowned and helped herself to toast.

'Yes,' Hilda nodded. 'She was devastated last time —goodness knows what this will do to her.'

'Was she my father's patient?'

'No, she's Dr Ashton's patient.' Hilda turned to the door, shaking her head over the heartache of the case, then paused. 'Are you taking surgery this morning, Alison?'

'Yes, Hilda, I am. Has Gill arrived?'

'I think I heard her come in a few minutes ago— she'll be sorting the post.'

'Good, I'll go and see her.' Alison stood up and, taking her toast and coffee with her and ignoring Hilda's look of disapproval, she made her way to the front of the house and the secretary's office.

'Alison!' Gill looked up with a wide smile from the mountain of post on her desk. 'Am I glad to see you! I think Dr Ashton would have snapped if he'd gone on on his own for much longer.'

'Oh, I don't know, Gill. I think it would take quite

a bit to make Grant Ashton snap,' Alison pulled a face.

'Well, you know what I mean.' Gill shrugged. 'So, where is he this morning?'

'Out on a call. A Mrs Cotton, according to Hilda.'

'Paula Cotton?' Gill looked up quickly.

'I don't know. Dubbers Farm?'

'Yes, that's her. Oh, God, I hope it's not another miscarriage?'

Alison shook her head. 'We'll have to wait and see. I don't think I know the Cottons. How long have they been at Dubbers?'

'Only about three years. They're into organic farming. Bob Cotton and his brother run the farm and Paula runs the farm shop. . .' Gill paused as the phone rang then rolled her eyes as she answered it.

'No,' she said into the mouthpiece, 'you wouldn't be able to see Dr Ashton this morning. But you can see Dr Kennedy. No, Dr Alison Kennedy. Yes. Yes, she is a doctor.' She grinned at Alison. Nine forty-five, then? Good. Your name? And the address? Thank you. Nine forty-five then, with Dr Kennedy.'

She smiled at Alison and replaced the receiver then, as the phone rang again immediately, she pulled a face. 'The word's got round—they'll be arriving in droves, you'll see.'

'In that case, I'd better get myself organised.' Alison drained her coffee-cup and strolled to the door, then as Gill's hand hovered over the receiver again she said, 'I'll be in my father's room, Gill.'

'Yes. OK.' Gill blinked, then, her voice suddenly husky, said, 'Good luck, Alison.'

Alison was forced to swallow the lump that had unexpectedly risen in her throat and she could only nod in response.

To her relief Hilda appeared to have been at work in the consulting room, or maybe it had been Gill—it didn't matter, for whoever it was had removed the sailing jacket from behind the door, replaced the blotter and notepads on the desk and put out clean laundry. The array of instruments was the same and the black case that had been her father's was waiting for her to use, but Alison was happy with that and wouldn't have had it any other way.

Ten minutes later as she sat down behind the desk she heard Grant return. She looked up, half expecting him to come into her room. Instead he went straight to his own room and closed the door and moments later she heard the sound of his buzzer indicating to Gill that he was ready for his first patient. She realised she had been hoping that he would come into her room, hoping that he too might have wished her luck on her first morning, as Gill had done. But why should he? Angrily she gave herself a little shake. There was no way she could expect any preferential treatment from Grant purely on the strength of their past acquaintance. And after all it had been she who had stipulated that theirs be a strictly professional relationship.

Almost savagely she pressed her intercom button.

'Gill? Would you ask my first patient to come in, please?'

'Certainly, Dr Kennedy.'

Two minutes later someone knocked at her open

door and as Alison glanced up she had to suppress a smile as Seth Attrill appeared.

'I heard you were back, Miss Alison.' He nodded in satisfaction. 'Or should I call you Dr Kennedy now?' Not waiting for her reply, he went on, 'I found it a bit difficult at first, thinking of you as a doctor, but now I know that's what you are I find it easier. Now my missus, on the other hand, says she's coming to see you because she never could talk to a man about personal things—you know, Doctor, women's troubles and all that.'

'Yes, Seth, I know,' Alison replied solemnly.

'So she's made an appointment, and she'll be along to see you this afternoon. So between us, Doctor, we're pretty glad you've come back to Fairacre.'

'You know something, Seth?' She smiled as he came right into the room and sat down. 'So am I.'

CHAPTER FIVE

ALISON worked steadily through the list of patients and by the end of the morning she was left with a definite sense of satisfaction. The patients on the whole had seemed delighted to see her, and most of them had seemed to accept the situation and had even assumed she had permanently taken over her father's role. In the end she'd given up trying to explain that she might only be there for a trial period. As Sue came through on the intercom and informed her that there were no further patients for her to see, she sighed and leaned back in her chair, flexing her fingers and relaxing.

Her moment of respite was short-lived, however, as there came a short rap on the door and Grant strode into the room. He was grim-faced and for one moment Alison thought he was angry with her. Instinctively she sat up straight in her chair and stared at him.

'I think we should get into the habit of having a brief practice meeting after morning surgery each day so that we can liaise and make any necessary decisions,' he said abruptly.

'Yes, of course.' She frowned, wondering at his manner, still imagining that his abruptness was in some way directed at her.

'One thing I hadn't mentioned to you,' he went on, not giving her a chance to question him, 'was that at the present time we don't have a practice nurse. Jenny is on maternity leave and won't be back for at least a couple more months. Are you happy to carry on without getting a temporary nurse?'

She nodded. 'I assume we have back-up from the community team?'

'Yes, plus the midwives, of course. Now, was there anything you wanted to discuss?'

'Not really.' She glanced up and saw that the dark brows were still drawn into an uncompromising line. 'Oh, yes, there was just one thing. . .'

'Yes?' He raised his eyebrows enquiringly.

'I noticed you have a computer in your room—is it just for your personal use or do you have plans to computerise the surgery?'

'I would very much like to computerise the surgery; in fact many plans had been discussed to update the practice in general. . .'

'Was my father in favour of computerisation?' She stared at him in amazement.

A flicker of a smile crossed his features then. 'Not exactly, but he saw the necessity for it.'

'So what other plans do you have?'

'I don't think there's a lot of point in discussing those at the present time, not until we're clear about the future of the practice. Now, Alison, if there isn't anything else, I'll get on with my house calls.' He turned to the door, then paused and looked back. 'Gill has drawn up an on-duty rota—I'll start today and take the pager with me.' He gave a curt nod then and disappeared from the room.

Thoughtfully Alison watched him go, still wondering at the apparent abruptness of his manner. Moments later Sue appeared in the open doorway.

'How did it go?' she asked with a sympathetic grin.

'Not too badly—in fact I've had rather a good morning.' Alison smiled back. 'I wouldn't say the same for everyone, though,' she added.

'What do you mean?' A frown crossed Sue's features.

'Well, Dr Ashton doesn't seem too happy.'

'Oh, you mustn't mind him,' said Sue quickly. 'He's always like that after an incident like this morning's.'

'What do you mean? I don't understand.'

'Didn't you hear him shut himself in his room when he came back from the Cottons'?'

'Yes...but...'

'He was upset. Paula had suffered another miscarriage. He's always like that. He's the same when one of his patients dies. We've all got used to it now...' She stared curiously at Alison. 'Were you thinking he was off with you?'

'It had crossed my mind.' Alison gave a wry smile.

'Oh, no, you mustn't think that. He's lovely really when you get to know him.' As she spoke Sue collected up the patients' records and swept from the room.

Alison watched her go. Sue was very new at Fairacre and it was obvious that she was unaware of Alison's previous relationship with Grant Ashton and of just how well she had known him. On the other hand Alison had never worked with Grant before and she had always been of the opinion that to know someone fully you needed to work with them.

With a sigh she stood up and began collecting her instruments together, packing them into her case. Sue had implied that Grant's mood that morning had all been to do with his patient's miscarriage, but Alison still felt there had been a coolness directed at herself.

This feeling persisted throughout her first week even though they quickly settled into a routine.

Grant seemed to spend very little time at Fairacre when he wasn't on duty. Alison had no idea where he went, neither did she feel inclined to ask, and he certainly offered no information. This arrangement suited her, however, for when he was there she invariably found the atmosphere tense and strained. Their only daily contact seemed to be at meals and at the brief practice discussion each day following morning surgery.

Then, on Grant's day off, Alison was coming to the end of an afternoon surgery when she saw that the last patient on the list was registered with him.

'Come in, Mrs Dawson.' She looked up and smiled as a pale, tired-looking woman in her early fifties came into her consulting-room.

'Good afternoon, Dr Kennedy.' The woman looked apprehensive. 'I hope you don't mind my coming to see you.'

'Why should I?' Alison glanced at the woman's records. 'I see you're registered with Dr Ashton, but that doesn't matter. For urgent matters we will see each other's patients.'

Mrs Dawson looked uneasy and bit her lip. 'It's not really what you'd call an urgent matter, Doctor—not exactly a matter of life and death—but it's not something I feel I could discuss with a man.'

'So why don't you tell me about it?' said Alison.

'Well, it's since I started my change—everything just seems to be wrong, if you get my meaning.'

'When did you stop your periods, Mrs Dawson?'

'About a year ago, but it's been in the last few months that the problems have started.'

'Go on.'

'Well, for a start, I'm so tired that I hardly know what to do with myself. I'm awake every night—sometimes three or four times a night.'

'Do you know what wakes you?'

'Yes, hot flushes—they're dreadful, Doctor, one after another—they wake me up and I'll be soaked with sweat, so hot that sometimes I have to get up and get into a cool bath. Then I go back to bed only for it all to happen again a couple of hours later—I tell you, Dr Kennedy, I'm worn out with it all.'

'And do you get these flushes during the day?'

'Oh, yes, one after another sometimes—I'm sure the customers must notice.'

'Customers?'

'At the newsagents—I work there part-time.'

'I see,' said Alison, then gently, because Mrs Dawson was beginning to look upset, she added, 'Do you have any other symptoms?'

Mrs Dawson hesitated. 'It's hard to explain really but sometimes I feel so low... In the middle of the night when I wake up I could cry and cry for no reason...and at other times I seem to have lost all my confidence...'

'Have you discussed this at all with Dr Ashton?' asked Alison quietly.

The woman looked down at her hands. 'Not

really...I started to, once...I was going to tell him that my relationship with my husband hasn't been as good as it used to be—you know what I mean?' She looked anxious and when Alison nodded she went on, 'But in the end I couldn't. I was too embarrassed. Besides, I don't think men understand—how can they?' She paused. 'Take my husband, for instance; he doesn't understand... He doesn't know how I feel... The other night for example...'

She hesitated and Alison looked up. 'Go on—what happened?'

'There was a programme on the telly about this HRT and my husband said it was all a load of rubbish. He said women had always managed in the past so why should this generation be any different.'

'But that wouldn't necessarily be Dr Ashton's opinion,' said Alison.

Mrs Dawson shrugged and looked at her hands again.

'I'm sure if you were to discuss it with him you'd be surprised,' said Alison firmly. 'Dr Ashton may be a man, but he's also a doctor and he's used to dealing with problems like this.'

Mrs Dawson shook her head doubtfully. 'I still don't think I could discuss it with him... I'd be embarrassed...' She was silent for a moment then she looked up hopefully. 'Would you give me a prescription for this HRT, Dr Kennedy?'

'Well, Mrs Dawson——' Alison took a deep breath '—I'd like to, because I am a great believer in hormone replacement therapy.' She hesitated. 'Do you know what it actually does?'

'Vaguely—but I didn't understand everything they said on the programme,' said Mrs Dawson slowly.

'It replaces the hormones, mainly oestrogen, that your body stops producing when you reach your menopause,' explained Alison. 'It reduces the hot flushes and night sweats, helps control mood swings and depression, and it also helps to prevent a disease called osteoporosis, or thinning of the bones, that many women suffer as they get older—there's also recent evidence that it may protect against heart disease.'

'So you're in favour of it, then, Doctor? You don't think we should just grin and bear it?'

Alison smiled. 'I happen to think that great strides have been made in helping women to cope with what for some can be a distressing time, and it is a pity if we don't take advantage of what is available. But having said that, Mrs Dawson——' she hesitated '—you are not my patient, and I really don't think Dr Ashton would be too pleased if I were to start you off on a course of hormone replacement therapy without his knowledge.'

Mrs Dawson's face dropped in disappointment. 'In that case I might as well go.' Wearily she stood up. 'I'm sorry I've wasted your time, Doctor.'

'Sit down, Mrs Dawson,' replied Alison firmly. 'You haven't wasted my time. What I was going to suggest was that you should make an appointment to see Dr Ashton——'

'What's the point? I couldn't explain it properly; I'd be too embarrassed—that's why I came to you.'

'But if you like,' Alison continued, ignoring the woman's comments, 'I will have a word with him first and tell him what you've told me.'

'Would you really?' Mrs Dawson stared at her, her anxious expression lifted, and there was almost eagerness in her eyes. 'That would be great. I always get tongue-tied when I go to see him and I end up never telling him half of what I meant to. . . Don't get me wrong; he's very nice and I'm sure he's a good doctor but, well. . .he's too good-looking by half,' Mrs Dawson muttered. 'It puts you right off your stroke.'

'I'll see what I can do.' Alison smiled.

Mrs Dawson stood up and walked to the door, where she paused and looked back. 'If he says no, could I change doctors?'

'That is your right, certainly,' replied Alison, 'but Dr Frampton's surgery is quite a distance away.'

'Oh, I wasn't meaning Dr Frampton—I meant could I change to you? I really like the idea of a lady doctor.'

'I'm only here on a temporary basis at the moment, Mrs Dawson,' replied Alison firmly.

'That's a pity.'

As Mrs Dawson left the room Alison gave a little shudder as she wondered what Grant would say if he knew that already one of his patients was contemplating transferring to her. With a sigh she stood up and stretched, then she picked up her mobile phone and her car keys and walked through to Gill's office.

'Any calls for me, Gill?' she asked.

Gill looked up. 'Only one house call, Alison—oh, and there was one call from the marina.'

'The marina?' Alison paused.

'Yes, apparently the mooring fee for Dr Kennedy's yacht is due.'

Alison stared at her. 'Do you know,' she said slowly at last, 'I'd forgotten all about his boat?'

'It'll be yours now,' replied Gill quietly.

'Yes, I suppose so.' Alison glanced at her watch. 'I'll make the house call, then I think I'll slip down to the marina, sort this out and check that the boat is all right. Do you know where the keys are?'

'Yes, your father always left a set here.' Gill reached behind her and, taking a bunch of keys from a hook on the notice-board, handed them to Alison.

Her house call was to a young mother and her new baby who had just been discharged from hospital. Alison found them in the capable hands of the community midwife and, after she had examined them both and found everything to be satisfactory, she left the house with a promise to return the following day.

Her route to the marina took her through a network of leafy lanes, between tall horse-chestnut trees adorned with pink or white candles, and hedgerows tumbling with thick, creamy blackthorn blossom. May was Alison's favourite month, but as she drew nearer to the marina she found memories crowding into her mind as she recalled other trips to her father's boat. Her entire childhood had been spent in or around water and messing about in boats, and after her mother had died when Alison was seven she had spent even more time in her father's company.

She hadn't, however, sailed for a long time, and as she parked the Rover at the rear of the marina buildings she felt a familiar tingle of excitement as she caught the tang of sea air and heard the cries of the gulls that circled the harbour.

But, as she left the car and walked along the boardwalk to where the yacht, *The Kittihawk*, was moored, other memories encroached, more painful feelings, the knowledge that she would never see her father at the helm again.

There was an air of loneliness about *The Kittihawk* as it bobbed gently on the water, tugging at its moorings as if it knew it had been abandoned.

Carefully Alison stepped aboard into the cockpit, then, unlocking the hatch, climbed down into the galley. Everything was neat and tidy and looked to be in good repair, and slowly she walked through the galley to the door of the main cabin.

She was looking round wondering whether she should be thinking of trying to sell *The Kittihawk* when to her amazement she heard a faint noise from the cabin. Her heart seemed to turn over as she stared at the closed door, thinking she must have imagined it. There couldn't be anyone in there; the hatch had been locked. Maybe the noise had come from outside.

But even as she reassured herself with the fact the noise came again, louder this time, leaving her in no doubt that there was indeed someone in the cabin.

Her first instinct was to turn and run. If there was someone in there it could only be an intruder, someone who had broken into the boat. But if it was an intruder she should surely investigate—this was her boat now. On the other hand, an intruder could be desperate, violent even if he was cornered.

The sensible thing to do would be to creep away and raise the alarm. But even as the idea crossed her mind the handle of the cabin door began to turn.

In desperation Alison looked wildly around and, grabbing the first thing that came to hand, which happened to be the boat's fire extinguisher, she pointed it at the door.

The door swung open and the figure of a man filled the space.

'All right,' Alison gasped, 'that's far enough!'

'Alison! What the hell. . .?' Grant Ashton stepped into the galley, staring at her in shocked amazement. He was wearing denims and no shirt, his dark hair was tousled, and he looked as if he'd been asleep.

'I thought you were an intruder,' she muttered weakly, relief flooding over her.

'I thought the same about you,' he replied, his expression grim. 'I woke up and heard someone moving about. There has been quite a bit of vandalism on the boats lately,' he went on, 'and I thought maybe I had unwelcome visitors.' He glanced warily at the fire extinguisher. 'Would you mind pointing that thing somewhere else? I don't fancy being covered in foam.'

'But what are you doing here?' Alison, feeling foolish, lowered the extinguisher, shaking her head in bewilderment. 'I don't understand—you said you were asleep. . .?'

He nodded and pushed the hair out of his eyes, the gesture somehow boyish. 'I was simply catching up— I was called out three times in the night.' He shrugged. 'I often come here.'

She stared at him. Could it be that he found her presence at Fairacre so unbearable that he even found it necessary to go elsewhere to sleep? Before she had the chance to ask he spoke again.

'I do have another reason for being here.'

'You do?' Her gaze flickered past him to the open door of the cabin and beyond to the bunk and the rumpled bedclothes. The sight stirred a memory, a memory of another time, a time when they had made love in that very cabin, a time that now seemed so far away that it was as if it had happened in another lifetime.

'I've been working on the boat,' he explained. 'I'd already started some repairs and re-painting when Miles was alive...' He trailed off, his gaze following hers.

For a moment neither of them spoke and Alison knew that Grant too was remembering how it had once been between them. Suddenly she became very aware of his nearness, then he half turned towards her.

'Alison...?'

'Yes...?' Wildly she looked at him and saw his eyes darken. Then, even as her pulse began to race, the blood pounding in her head, without any further warning he stepped towards her and, taking her face between his hands, stared down into her eyes in a kind of hungry desperation before bringing his lips down to cover hers in a hard, demanding kiss.

Instinctively Alison felt her whole body stiffen in defence, her arms rigid by her sides, her hands curled into tight fists.

This couldn't be happening. She couldn't let it happen again. It had nearly destroyed her before; this time she would stand no chance of survival.

She closed her eyes, squeezing them tightly shut so that she couldn't see the expression in those tantalising green eyes, wishing as she waited for him to release her that she could also shut down her sense of smell as she caught the once so familiar male scent of him.

But he hadn't finished, and as his kiss became more possessive, more demanding longings stirred deep inside her, longings denied and suppressed for so long that she had doubted they were still there.

Fiercely, expertly, he parted her lips with tongue and teeth then, moving his hands, which had become entangled in her hair, he ran them down over her body, drawing her roughly against his naked chest, the hardness of his own body leaving her in no doubt about his state of arousal.

This was madness. Sheer madness. As her feelings threatened to overwhelm her, to spiral out of control, Alison summoned a force of strength from somewhere and physically pushed him away.

For a moment they stared at each other, their breath coming fast, the passion still flaring between them.

'That was against the rules.' He gave a short, mocking laugh. 'It didn't quite fit your pattern of professional behaviour, did it?'

Then, not giving her a chance to reply, he gave a curt, dismissive gesture. 'Sorry, Alison. It shouldn't have happened. Forget it.' He turned away as if he too was fighting to regain control, then abruptly he half turned towards her, again running his fingers through his short dark hair, pushing it back from his forehead, and, as if it had only just occurred to him, he asked, 'What did you come here for?'

Leaning back, she gripped the edge of the worktop

for support, not wanting him to see how shaken she was.

'I. . .I . . . that is, Gill had a call from the marina to say the mooring fee was due. I thought I'd call in and pay it and check on the boat at the same time.' She glanced wildly round as she spoke, hoping he wouldn't notice that she was still shaking. 'It looks, however, as if you have everything under control.'

He shrugged. 'As I said, I'd already started painting and it seemed sensible to finish.'

'You'll have to let me have the bill,' she replied stiffly.

They stared at each other again for a long moment.

'There won't be any need for that, Alison,' he said at last, shaking his head, the gesture implying sadness that things should have come to that between them. 'But on the subject of *The Kittihawk*——' he hesitated '—I had wondered if you would consider selling her to me.'

'To you. . .' Her eyes widened.

'Is that so strange?'

'I thought you already had a boat.'

'I sold it recently. I've been looking for another—this would be ideal—she's special and she sails like a dream.'

Sell *The Kittihawk* to him? She frowned.

'Think about it,' he said lightly. 'I realise it isn't something you can decide immediately. . .'

The sudden sound of footsteps above them made them both look up.

Long, tanned legs descended the galley steps and, to Alison's amazement, Cheryl Rossi appeared, her sun-bleached hair a wild, tousled mass, glossy lips parted in a breathless smile.

'Oh, Grant,' she breathed, ignoring Alison, 'you are still here. I thought you might have gone.'

'Hello, Cheryl.' His gaze flickered to Alison. 'Alison's come to sort out the mooring fees for *The Kittihawk*.'

Cheryl turned her gaze on Alison. 'You'll need to see Ken Bridges about that,' she said. 'If you hurry you'll just about catch him before he goes home.' As she was speaking she hoisted herself on to the worktop. 'I'll stay and talk to you, Grant,' she added, crossing her slim ankles.

Alison hesitated, then abruptly she turned and climbed the galley steps, emerging thankfully into the late afternoon sunshine, but as she crossed the boardwalk the sound of Cheryl's laughter floated up from the galley of *The Kittihawk*.

Cheryl's sudden appearance had unnerved her, or maybe it had been what had happened between herself and Grant. Alison wasn't sure, but whatever it was she found that all she wanted was to get away from the boat as quickly as she could.

She found Ken Bridges in the marina office. He was a man in his early forties, bearded and of stocky build, and had spent his life in or around boats. His tanned face creased into a smile when he caught sight of her.

'Alison, it's good to see you again.'

'Hello, Ken. Cheryl said I'd find you here.'

He stood up, then winced as if in sudden pain before walking round to the front of his desk.

Alison narrowed her eyes. 'Are you having problems?'

'It's my back again.' He gave a forced smile. 'The wretched disc – it goes from time to time. I'll have to come up to Fairacre.' He paused. 'I understand you're doing your father's surgery?'

'That's right, Ken, I am.' Alison nodded. 'Give Sue a ring and make an appointment and we'll try and sort things out for you.'

'Thanks, Alison.' He looked relieved. 'Now, I'm sure you didn't come here to discuss my health.'

Alison laughed. 'Not really, Ken. I came to pay the mooring fee on *The Kittihawk*,' she said, taking her cheque-book from her bag.

'I see.' He turned to a metal cabinet and drew out a file. 'What are you going to do with her, Alison?'

'I don't know yet,' she replied. 'I haven't decided.'

He hesitated, then looked up from the file. 'I rather get the impression that Dr Ashton would like to buy her.'

'Yes, Ken, I get that impression as well,' she said briskly. 'But, as I said, I haven't decided what I want to do with her. I don't intend to be rushed into anything. I may well decide to keep her and sail her myself.'

'Good for you.' Ken chuckled and took the cheque she handed him. 'That sounds about what I'd expect from Miles Kennedy's daughter.'

CHAPTER SIX

'DAWSON, you say? Do you mean Brenda Dawson?' Grant frowned at her across his desk.

It was during their daily practice meeting and Alison had brought up the patient's name as she had promised.

'Yes, that's right. She came to see me and——'

'Wait a minute; let's get this straight. Brenda Dawson came to see you?'

'Yes, that's what I said——'

'But she's my patient.'

'I know she's your patient, Grant but——'

'So was it something urgent?'

'It was concerning her menopausal symptoms.'

'I'd hardly call that urgent.'

'No, Grant, maybe you wouldn't!' She glared at him, stung by his apparently abrupt attitude. 'But I rather imagine Brenda Dawson had reached the end of her tether! She came to me because I suspect she thought she might find more sympathy from another woman.' As Grant remained silent she swept on, refusing to be intimidated. 'She saw a recent programme on HRT and felt she might like to try it, but it would seem she didn't feel she could approach you.'

'She told you that?' He raised his eyebrows, his tone icy now.

'She didn't have to. I drew my own conclusions. But

I would have thought she was a prime candidate for replacement therapy.'

'Is that so?' Coolly he surveyed her and Alison found herself thinking of the brief flare-up of passion between them the previous day and wondered if she'd dreamt it. 'So did you prescribe it?'

She shook her head. 'No. I suggested that Mrs Dawson come back to see you——'

'But that you would have a word with me in the meantime on her behalf—am I right?'

She bit her lip and lowered her gaze, embarrassed by the accuracy of his assessment.

He leaned back in his chair and began toying with the brass paper-knife from his desk. 'So is that the end of today's lesson, Dr Kennedy?' he asked at last.

She flushed at the sarcasm in his tone and clenched her fists at her sides. 'I wasn't presuming to——' she began through gritted teeth, but he cut her short.

'Weren't you, Alison? I would say that's precisely what you were doing. Just for the record, Brenda Dawson has never mentioned her menopausal symptoms to me—if she had I would have suggested some measure of relief. But as it is I'm not a mind-reader —I can't suggest a remedy if I'm not told the condition —maybe you could pass that message on to her when she consults you again, as doubtless she now will.'

'Maybe your female patients find it difficult trying to explain problems of a certain nature within the confines of an ordinary daily surgery,' said Alison tightly, furious now at his attitude when all she had been doing was trying to help.

'I suppose you mean I should run a Well Woman clinic?' His eyes narrowed.

'Precisely,' she replied. 'I happen to believe they are invaluable for encouraging women to discuss problems they might otherwise feel inhibited about. I intend to re-start my father's clinic just as soon as I can get it going again, and it might not be a bad idea for you to do the same!' She glared at him across the desk.

'Have you quite finished?' He paused and she bit her lip. 'Not that it's any of your business, but just for the record, and quite apart from the fact that most women have difficulty getting to these daytime clinics because they work, I happen to believe the exact opposite to what you have just said.'

'What do you mean?' she demanded.

'From experience—and you have to admit that when it comes to general practice I do have a little more of that than you. . .' He inclined his head as he spoke and Alison drew in her breath sharply. 'From experience,' he went on smoothly, 'I have found that within the boundaries of a daily surgery I find out much more about women's problems that I would in a month of Sundays of specific clinics.'

'In that case it's a pity you didn't spot Brenda Dawson's problems!' she retorted, then, not giving him a chance for further retaliation, she turned and marched from the room, hating him for his arrogance, hating him for the emotional turmoil he had rekindled the day before when he had kissed her, wanting to hurt him, to retaliate in some way but powerless to know how to do so.

Her cheeks still stinging, she turned into the hall

and collided with Hilda who was standing on a stepladder, the hall curtains in her arms.

As the step-ladder wobbled precariously Hilda gave a cry of alarm and Alison gasped, reaching out and steadying the ladder. 'Oh, Hilda, I'm so sorry,' she said. 'I didn't see you there.'

'It's all right, no harm done.' Hilda stepped to the ground then peered at her. 'What's wrong, dear?'

'It's him,' Alison muttered. 'He's impossible!'

'I think this calls for a cup of tea,' replied Hilda firmly. 'Come on, dear, come through to the kitchen. I'll just put these curtains in the washing machine, then I'll put the kettle on.'

It was comfortable, safe, familiar in the kitchen with it's childhood memories—tea-towels drying over the Aga, jars of preserves, neatly labelled by Hilda and placed in rows on the top shelf of the dresser, and Marmaduke, the ginger tom, snoozing on the window-ledge in the sun.

Fighting sudden, angry tears, Alison flopped down into the rocking-chair beside the Aga and kicked off her shoes.

'Do you want to tell me about it?' Hilda bustled about loading the washing machine. 'Or is it confi?'

In spite of herself Alison smiled. In the past 'confi' had always been their pet name for practice business of a confidential nature.

'No, Hilda,' she sighed, reaching up and stroking Marmaduke, who stirred at her touch then stretched and re-curled himself more comfortably, 'not really. At least, I suppose the reason for today's argument was confi, but it's not just that. I really don't think this whole thing is going to work.'

'I thought things seemed to be going rather well.' Hilda shut the door of the machine then took the kettle to the sink. 'You must admit it's been quiet the last week.'

'Only because we haven't seen too much of each other. Did you know, Hilda, he's been sleeping on the boat?'

'On the boat!' Hilda looked startled.

'Yes, I found him on *The Kittihawk* catching up on his sleep.'

'But why should he do that?'

Alison shrugged. 'Search me. I can only imagine he wants to avoid me.'

Hilda, about to spoon tea into the teapot, paused and looked at her. As she continued pouring boiling water on to the tea she mused. 'Maybe he's remembering another relationship.'

'What do you mean?' Alison looked up sharply at Hilda's change of tone, but the older woman now appeared to be struggling to open a packet of digestive biscuits.

'Maybe he finds this type of relationship difficult after the one you once had,' Hilda said at last, emptying the biscuits on to a plate.

'That's his problem!' Alison retorted, then, catching sight of Hilda's reproachful expression, she added, 'I'm sorry, Hilda, but it is. I know things were different between us once, but that was a long time ago. We are two entirely different people now—there's no going back to what might have been.'

'Are you sure of that, love?' Hilda smiled and handed her a cup of tea.

'Quite sure, Hilda.'

'And are you sure Dr Ashton feels like that as well?'

'Of course he does. I still feel that he used me, Hilda. I could never trust him again.'

Hilda stirred her tea thoughtfully. 'Just supposing he didn't use you, love? Supposing what happened wasn't his fault?'

'What do you mean?' Alison demanded. 'He did use me, Hilda, and in my book that's enough.' Draining her cup, she struggled to her feet. 'That was nice, but this won't do. I have patients to see. Thanks, Hilda, see you later.' Purposefully she strode from the kitchen and, grabbing her case from her consulting-room, she collected her pile of patient records from Gill and marched to her car.

Before she turned on the ignition she sat for a moment reflecting on her conversation with Hilda. It was common knowledge that Hilda thought the world of her. She had, after all, been around for most of Alison's growing up and it had also been common knowledge that she had been devoted to Dr Kennedy, but what was becoming increasingly obvious to Alison since her return to Fairacre was Hilda's affection for Grant Ashton.

Hilda had probably assumed that on Alison's return the relationship between her and Grant would carry on where it had left off around four years ago. Alison hoped that now she had put paid to any such assumptions. It simply couldn't be the same, no matter how sentimental Hilda was about the past. The clock couldn't be turned back. The two people she and Grant had once been simply no longer existed.

'Are you going to sit there all day?'

A voice cut into her thoughts, and she looked up sharply to see Grant leaning on the open door of his car apparently waiting for her to move.

Because she had been thinking about him, fantasising really, her heart seemed to turn over and, imagining him able to read her thoughts, she felt the colour flood her cheeks.

With a muttered apology and only too aware of his look of amused exasperation she shot her car into gear, let out the clutch too quickly and stalled the engine. Unable to look at Grant again, she re-started the engine and, conscious that he was still watching her, drove smartly away.

During the evening of the following day Alison received a telephone call from Bob Cotton at Dubbers Farm.

'Sorry to bother you at this hour, Dr Kennedy,' he said, 'but is Dr Ashton on duty?'

'No, not this evening, I'm afraid,' she replied. 'Can I be of any help?'

'Well——' he hesitated '——it's my wife, Paula. She had a miscarriage recently and she was discharged from hospital a couple of days ago. But she's not at all well, Dr Kennedy.'

'In what way?'

'Hard to say really; she just isn't herself, if you know what I mean. She's very depressed. . .'

'That's understandable.'

'I know, but it's more than that, Doctor, if you get my meaning. I can't put my finger on it but she's just not right.'

'All right, Mr Cotton, I'll come over and see her,' said Alison. Thoughtfully she replaced the receiver then walked to the filing cabinet and pulled out Paula Cotton's records.

Half an hour later she drew up in the yard of Dubbers Farm to be greeted by a flurry of hens and the frantic barking of two Border collies.

She liked Bob Cotton on sight. His face was open, his handshake warm, but his eyes were full of anxiety as he showed her into the bedroom. His wife Paula, a pretty, dark-haired woman, was propped up in bed; her face appeared red and blotchy and her eyes were swollen from crying.

'Hello, Mrs Cotton—Paula.' Alison sat down on the side of the double bed. 'I was so sorry to hear about your miscarriage,' she added, coming straight to the point.

Paula's eyes filled with tears and she shook her head as if she couldn't bring herself to speak.

'I see from your records,' said Alison, glancing up at Bob Cotton who was hovering anxiously near the door, 'that this was your third miscarriage. Your first one was when you were living in Northamptonshire, is that correct?'

Paula nodded and wiped her eyes with a tissue.

'Were you given any reason?'

It was Bob who answered. 'Only that it's nature's way sometimes to abort an unhealthy foetus. We accepted that—we were upset, naturally, but we accepted it—we even accepted it the second time, but now. . .well, three times is a bit hard to take. . .'

'I agree,' replied Alison quietly. 'Now, the second time I see happened soon after you arrived here.'

'Yes, we'd only just bought the farm and we'd just registered with Dr Ashton—he's been very good through all this,' Bob added hastily. 'He organised lots of tests for Paula, I don't want you to think we've called you out for a second opinion or anything like that, Dr Kennedy.'

'I know you haven't; you didn't know Dr Ashton wasn't on call,' Alison reasured him.

'It's just that Paula's been feeling so wretched since she came home from the hospital, haven't you, love?' Bob Cotton glanced down at his wife.

'I see from your discharge summary that you've had a D and C,' remarked Alison.

'Yes.' Paula nodded, speaking for the first time. 'Yes, they said it was an incomplete abortion and my womb needed clearing.'

'Right. Now do you have a follow-up appointment with the gynaecologist?'

'Yes, he said he would discuss my history with me then.'

'Well, hopefully they will do further tests, Paula, and discover why you are unable to carry a baby full-term,' said Alison gently.

'Something has to be done,' said Bod Cotton helplessly. 'We can't go on like this. But in the meantime, Doctor, why is Paula feeling so bad? Can you give her something just until we see Dr Ashton again?'

'Did they prescribe anything for you at the hospital, Paula?' asked Alison.

'Only pain-killers and sleeping tablets,' Paula replied.

'In that case I'd like to take your blood-pressure, your pulse and your temperature and listen to your chest.'

After Alison had satisfied herself that all seemed normal with Paula apart from slightly raised blood-pressure, she asked if she had felt unwell between her pregnancies.

'Not really,' Paula replied. 'I felt really dreadful each time from the moment I knew I was pregnant, and at the time of the miscarriages, but it died down in between.'

'When you say dreadful, what exactly do you mean?' asked Alison.

'Tired, Doctor, so tired I could hardly think and sometimes I had a pain in my chest and my joints ached.' Again her eyes filled with tears.

'I think at the moment, Paula, you are very low after losing your baby,' said Alison. 'More tests will have to be done, of course, but in the meantime I'll prescribe a short course of antidepressants. Take things very quietly until you have your follow-up appointment, then I'm sure Dr Ashton will be wanting to see you again.'

Alison was in a thoughtful mood as she drove back to Fairacre. It was tragic for Paula and Bob Cotton to have lost three babies and, while she didn't doubt that Grant was doing all he could, she found herself wondering if there could be rather more wrong with Paula than there seemed.

There was no sign of Grant's car and the house was quiet, the garden hushed in the softness of the May evening.

Deep purple lilac tumbled over the wall, a laburnum glowed in the corner by the brick archway that led to the rear gardens, and wisteria crept over the front porch.

Alison paused for a moment, enjoying the stillness, realising that in spite of all the trauma she really was pleased to be back at Fairacre.

The front door was closed, the surgeries long over for the day. Gill would have gone home and Hilda would be in her room watching her favourite soap opera. Wearily Alison turned the handle and pushed open the door; maybe she would have time for a quick shower before the phone rang again. . .

'Alison. . .is that you. . .?'

The voice was faint, weak, not instantly recognisable, and she paused, the door still open, and glanced round. For one instant the overturned chair beneath the hall window had no significance, then her gaze flew to the figure huddled on the floor.

'Hilda!' With a cry she hurried forward.

'Oh, Alison! Thank goodness you've come. I didn't know what to do.' Hilda was half submerged by the freshly laundered hall curtains. Her glasses lay beside her on the floor. 'I can't move, you see—I've hurt my leg.'

'It's all right, Hilda—just lie still.' Quickly Alison

removed the curtains, noting as she did so the grotesque angle of Hilda's right leg. Automatically she took the older woman's pulse, noting its rapidity, then expertly but gently she examined her, running her hands over her hips and legs.

'It was so silly,' said Hilda weakly. 'I was only putting the curtains back—I don't know what happened.'

'Why weren't you using the step-ladder, Hilda?'

'I don't like it; it wobbles. I feel much safer on a chair.'

'Oh, Hilda,' murmured Alison, then hurried into her consulting-room, returning a moment later with a blanket. 'Do you know where Dr Ashton is?' she asked as gently she covered Hilda.

'I think he said he was going to the boat. . .'

'I see; well, I'm going to phone the hospital.'

'Oh, that won't be necessary, dear, I shall be fine in a few minutes—perhaps you could get me a cup of tea, then I expect I'll be able to get up. . .' Hilda trailed off and gasped in sudden pain.

'I'm sorry, Hilda, but I'm afraid this is one thing that won't be cured by a cup of tea,' said Alison. 'In fact, I can't even give you a drink.'

'Oh!' Hilda's face fell.

'I think you may have broken your hip, Hilda. If so, the hospital will need to give you an anaesthetic. I can't let you have anything to eat or drink. Now just lie still while I go and phone.'

Hilda sighed and leaned back against the cushion Alison had propped under her head.

In her consulting-room Alison dialled the number of the general hospital and asked to speak to the casualty officer. She waited a few moments, wishing that Grant would come home.

'Hello, Dr Kennedy?' A heavily accented voice finally spoke from the other end of the line. 'Rajiv Patel here. How can I help you?'

'Ah, Dr Patel, I have a lady here with, I suspect, a fractured neck of femur,' replied Alison. 'I'd like to bring her into Casualty.'

'Of course. I'll arrange an ambulance. Who is the patient?'

'Her name is Hilda Lloyd.'

'Is she your patient?'

'Actually she's a friend; she lives with us here at Fairacre. . .' She paused as for the first time it dawned on her that Hilda was in fact now her patient as she had been registered with her father. 'And yes,' she added, 'she is my patient as well.'

'Very well, I will expect her shortly. Will you accompany her?'

'I hope to, but I'm on call here in Woodbridge and I'm not sure whether I can contact Dr Ashton to take over.'

She hung up and immediately re-dialled the number of Grant's mobile phone. As she waited she prayed he hadn't switched it off, but it was more than likely that he had, as he wasn't on call.

She counted the rings—seven, eight, nine—and was about to hang up when Grant suddenly answered. He sounded breathless, as if he'd been running.

'Grant?'

'Alison, what is it?'

'It's Hilda; she's had a fall. I think she's fractured

her hip. I'm waiting for the ambulance.'

'I'm on my way,' he replied.

In the second before the line went dead Alison heard another voice, a woman's voice, and briefly she wondered if it was Cheryl. Cheryl had been on the boat before. Then she dismissed the thought. It wasn't anything to do with her who Grant spent his time with when he was off duty, and she had no way of knowing whether it had been Cheryl's voice she had heard—come to that, she had no way of knowing whether Grant had even been on the boat. Hilda had thought he had gone there, but he could have been anywhere. . .

She bit her lip, then she shrugged and hurried back to the hall, where she talked to Hilda, comforting and calming her while they waited.

Grant arrived first. His eyes met Alison's as he strode into the house, then he crouched beside Hilda.

'What have you been up to?' he said softly.

'It was so silly,' whispered Hilda, shaking her head. Already shock was setting in and she looked pale and drawn.

Gently Grant lifted back the blanket and ran his hands lightly over Hilda's hips, then he glanced up and as his gaze met Alison's again he gave a slight nod, confirming her diagnosis.

'You're not to worry, Hilda,' he said, covering her again then taking hold of her hand and chafing it between his own. 'We'll soon have you in hospital.'

Even as he spoke there came the sound of tyres outside on the drive.

'Here's the ambulance.' Alison scrambled to her

feet. 'I'll go and get a nightie and a toothbrush for you, Hilda.'

Leaving Grant to assist the paramedics, she hurried upstairs to Hilda's room where she quickly packed a small bag. When she returned she found they had lifted Hilda into the ambulance.

'Grant. . .?' Alison stood back then looked enquiringly at him as he climbed from the back of the ambulance, wondering who should go with Hilda, desperately wanting to go herself but only too aware that she was on call.

'I'll do the on-call,' he said briefly, as if he was able to read her thoughts. 'You go with Hilda.'

'Thank you, Grant.' For a long moment her gaze met his and she saw the understanding in his eyes. 'Thank you,' she whispered again before climbing into the back of the ambulance.

CHAPTER SEVEN

HILDA'S examination and X-rays showed her to have a fractured neck of femur. Alison stayed with her while she was admitted to an orthopaedic ward, only preparing to leave as she was being taken to Theatre.

'You'll be all right, Hilda.' Alison kissed her cheek. 'They'll be keeping you in for a while. I'll come in some time tomorrow to see you.'

'Don't you worry about me.' Hilda sounded drowsy from her pre-med. 'You get back to Dr Ashton; he'll be wanting his supper. Now, don't you two fight now that I'm not there, will you?'

'Oh, Hilda, as if we would!' Alison pulled a face.

She felt tired on her drive back to Fairacre and thought she might go straight to bed, but as she opened the front door Grant came out of the kitchen.

'How is she?' he asked.

'In Theatre,' she replied briefly, then added, 'As we thought, fractured neck of femur—a nasty break apparently.'

'Poor Hilda—she'll be out of action for some time. How was she taking it?'

'She was in pain, but her biggest concern seemed to be that you would be wanting your supper,' she told him drily.

He gave a grimace. 'I think Hilda's of the opinion that I'm totally unable to care for myself.'

'And are you?'

'Judge for yourself.' He stood back and with a flourish indicated for her to enter the kitchen.

Alison walked slowly towards the door, then on the threshold stopped in surprise. Two places were laid at the large table and a wooden bowl of fresh salad had been placed in the centre.

'Not only am I able to care for myself,' he commented, 'but I've also prepared supper for you. I hope you like Spanish omelettes?'

'Love them,' she replied weakly, then sank down on to the nearest chair.

'Good.' He crossed to the food mixer and switched it on. 'Glass of wine?'

'Yes, please.' She sighed, content for the moment to let him take control, and watched as he poured a glass of red wine. Although he was on call he'd changed into casual wear—denims and a rust-coloured sweatshirt—and she guessed he'd just taken a shower because his hair was still damp.

'I'm not surprised it was a bad break,' he said, raising the gas flame under the frying-pan and switching off the food mixer, 'I once heard your father say that Hilda had mild osteoporosis.'

'Pity there was no hormone replacement therapy around when she was younger.' Alison took a sip of her wine.

Grant turned from the stove and raised his eyebrows. 'Is that another dig at me because of Brenda Dawson?'

'Of course not, I wouldn't dream of it.'

'Good. I don't think it would be the thing to start arguing now, do you?'

'That was the other thing Hilda was worried about.'

'Oh?' He paused, the frying-pan in one hand. 'What do you mean?'

'She was worried we would fight if we were left alone.'

He grinned. 'I don't know what ever gave her that idea.'

She sighed again, leaned back in her chair, and watched him as he finished cooking the omelettes.

'Have there been any other calls?' she asked suddenly, remembering that he had taken over her duty.

He shook his head and transferred the omelettes to plates that had been warming on the Aga. 'No, for once it was quiet—just one request for advice. Now, let's forget the practice for a while and enjoy our supper.' He set one plate down in front of her and the other opposite, then took his own place at the table.

The food was delicious and as she began to eat Alison realised how hungry she was. 'Well, at least I shall be able to reassure Hilda that you can cook,' she remarked.

'The ability to cook isn't the problem,' he said thoughtfully; 'it's finding the time to do so.'

'Do you think we should get anyone else while Hilda is recovering?' Alison glanced up from her plate.

'Shall we see if we can manage—at least for the time being, until we know what's happening?'

'What do you mean?' She frowned.

He gave a slight shrug and put down his knife and fork. 'Well, I think we have to face up to the fact that Hilda isn't getting any younger, and after what has happened today there's a very good chance she won't be able to work. I used to worry about the amount she was doing as it was, but when I suggested she might want to take things a little easier she got very upset and I didn't broach the matter again.' As he pushed his plate away the phone rang and he sighed. 'I thought it was too good to be true,' he muttered.

Alison half stood up but he motioned to her to sit down again. 'I'll take it,' he said.

'But it's me on duty,' she protested.

'I'll do tonight.' He stood up and walked to the door.

'But that's not fair on you—it's my turn.'

'Don't worry,' he grinned, 'you can do one for me in return.'

Alison sighed, and as Grant disappeared she gazed round the kitchen. Little more than a month ago she had been happy at the Crandelbury Street practice where her future prospects had looked good, her father had been alive and running the Fairacre practice with Grant, and Hilda had been caring for the two men— now her beloved father had gone, her dreams of a partnership in Suffolk had been put on hold, and Hilda, poor Hilda who had cared for her since she was a child, was lying injured in hospital.

A wave of self-pity and loneliness engulfed her, her eyes filled with tears and, to her dismay, Grant chose that precise moment to return.

'It's OK,' he was saying as he came into the kitchen, 'only another one for advice. . .' He trailed off as he caught sight of her face. 'What is it?' His tone softened.

'Oh, it's nothing.' She shrugged and drew the back of her hand hastily across her eyes, not wanting him to see her tears.

'You don't cry for nothing, Ali,' he said gently, moving round behind her. 'I know you, remember?'

She remembered—only too well. 'I wasn't crying,' she retorted hastily.

'Then why were your eyes full of tears?' He had stopped behind her chair.

'I don't know. It was just...just...well, first it was Dad, now it's Hilda...I suppose it just got to me, that's all...the tension built up.'

'Troubles never do come singly.' He placed his hands on her shoulders and at his touch she stiffened. 'But tension can be dealt with.' Gently but firmly his strong fingers began massaging the nape of her neck. 'Come on, Ali, relax. If you don't bend soon, you'll snap.'

Still she sat rigid, resisting his touch, unable to let her guard slip.

'Besides, we have to get along; we mustn't fight—it would upset Hilda.' He gave a low chuckle while his thumbs moved lower, easing out the hard knot of tension between her shoulderblades.

Gradually, in spite of her reluctance to let him see just how vulnerable she was, she felt herself begin to relax as the accumulated stress of the last few weeks began to ebb away.

With a sigh she leaned back, and even when she realised that her head was resting against his thigh she was happy to let it remain, while his hands continued to heal.

He'd done this once before, she thought dreamily, on one of her visits home when she had been uptight about exams. On that occasion also he had relaxed her, eased away her tension...

'There,' he murmured soothingly at last, rousing her slightly from her state of reverie. 'Is that feeling better?'

'Mmm, yes—yes, that's lovely.' She stretched, lifting her arms above her head. 'And it beats fighting.'

'Oh, I don't know.' He leaned forward so that he was looking down at her upturned face. 'The best bit about fighting is the making up afterwards...but I can't imagine why Hilda thought we would fight anyway if we were alone... After all, it wouldn't be the first time we'd been left alone in this house, would it?'

As he was speaking he tilted her chair back slightly so that it was resting against him, then he encircled her face with his hands, imprisoning her. 'Surely, Ali, you haven't forgotten the last time?'

How could she forget? Helplessly she stared up at him and even though he was upside-down she could detect the spark of humour in his green eyes.

Relentlessly he went on. 'If I remember rightly, it was while your father was attending a conference in Birmingham and Hilda's sister went down with flu. I am right, aren't I? Correct me if I'm wrong. But I certainly don't recall any fighting; what I do recall is Hilda spending two nights in Bembridge with her sister and the two of us having Fairacre to ourselves.' His tone softened as with deadly accuracy he reconstructed the past.

'The first night was very warm, and around midnight we took a stroll through the copse—by then it had become our special place. There was a little hollow in the bank and if you found the right spot it was very comfortable. Mind you, we weren't too bothered about comfort in those days, were we, Ali?'

Leaning over, he kissed the tip of her nose. 'We weren't even too bothered when, on the following evening, the leg on your bed gave way——' He gave a wicked chuckle. 'I managed to get that repaired without your father ever knowing. And now—who would have thought it?—after all this time here we are again in a similar situation—could it be time to revive some of those old memories, to see if it was all as good as we thought it was, to see if the old magic is still there. . .?'

It would be so easy. Lulled by his voice, she too relived the past, the excitement of the two nights they had spent alone, that hour at midnight in the soft grass of the copse. For one crazy moment she could feel his arms around her again, his naked skin against hers, the weight of his body, the taste of his kisses. . .

'Alison,' he whispered urgently.

With a supreme effort she jerked upright, pulling away from him. 'No, Grant!' She stood up and moved away from him, angry that she had put herself in such a vulnerable position. 'It's over. It was over a long time ago. You know that. There's no point in trying to drag it all up again.'

'For a moment there I thought it might have been what you wanted. . .'

'But why? Why again?'

'We are different people now; you are older for a start. . .'

'Are you implying I wasn't grown-up?' she demanded, her eyes widening.

'I didn't say that——'

'I seem to remember I was grown-up enough for some things.' Her anger began to mount as she faced him, recalling how hurt she had been. 'Besides, it was you who said you hadn't meant to get serious—you who ended it... You used me, Grant!'

'No, Ali,' he sighed. 'Never that...but you never really understood...I never had the chance to explain.'

'There was nothing to explain...'

'That's all you know about it,' he said ruefully.

'It's no good. It's too late, Grant,' she said firmly. 'And if we go on like this we really will end up fighting. Now, if you're quite happy to be on call, I'm going to bed.'

He didn't reply, and when she reached the door she paused and looked back. He was still standing where she had left him, leaning back against the worktop.

'Grant?'

'Yes?'

'Are you happy to do the on-call?'

'I said so, didn't I?' His voice was bleak again—the tenderness of only moments earlier gone now.

She swallowed. 'Thank you.'

He was still in the kitchen when she reached her bedroom. She shut the door, then, closing her eyes, she leaned against it for a moment.

He'd indicated that he wanted to resume their relationship. But how could she? Supposing he did the same thing to her again? She had recovered last time, but only just; next time he might destroy her.

He had wanted to explain. But what was there to

GET 4 BOOKS
A CUDDLY TEDDY
AND A MYSTERY GIFT

FREE

Return this card, and we'll send you 4 Mills & Boon romances, absolutely FREE! We'll even pay the postage and packing for you!

We're making you this offer to introduce to you the benefits of Mills & Boon Reader Service: FREE home delivery of brand-new Mills & Boon romances, at least a month before they're available in the shops, FREE gifts and a monthly Newsletter packed with special offers and information.

Accepting these FREE books places you under no obligation to buy, you may cancel at any time, even after receiving just your free shipment.

Yes, please send me 4 free Mills & Boon romances, a cuddly teddy and a mystery gift as explained above. Please also reserve a Reader Service subscription for me. If I decide to subscribe, I shall receive 6 superb new titles every month for just £11.40 postage and packing free. If I decide not to subscribe I shall write to you within 10 days. The free books and gifts will be mine to keep in any case. I understand that I am under no obligation whatsoever. I may cancel or suspend my subscription at any time simply by writing to you.

Ms/Mrs/Miss/Mr _____ 10A4R

Address _____

_____ Postcode _____

Signature _____
I am over 18 years of age.

Get 4 books a cuddly teddy and mystery gift FREE!

SEE BACK OF CARD FOR DETAILS

Mills & Boon Reader Service,
FREEPOST
P.O. Box 236
Croydon
CR9 9EL

Offer expires 30th April 1995. One per household. The right is reserved to refuse an application and change the terms of this offer. Offer applies to U.K. and Eire only. Offer not available for current subscribers to Mills & Boon romances. Readers overseas please send for details. Southern Africa write to: IBS Private Bag X3010, Randburg 2125. You may be mailed with offers from other reputable companies as a result of this application. If you would prefer not to receive such offers, please tick this box.

No stamp needed

explain? He had used her, then tired of her. It was as simple as that.

Now, she thought as she slowly undressed, at all costs she had to resist him. To resist him even if her body played treacherous games when he was near.

But later, as she lay wakeful in her bed and heard the creak of the stairs as he came up to his own room, it took every ounce of will-power not to go to him. . . To slip into bed beside him, to turn to him as she had before, then to have him love her, love her as only he could, as no other man had done since.

Finally, as the house fell silent, with a sigh she turned her face to the wall.

Like the early morning breeze that rippled through the apple blossom, the coolness was back between them. By the time Alison came downstairs Grant had finished his toast and coffee and was on the way to his surgery.

'Good night?' she enquired as they passed in the kitchen doorway.

'Very, thanks—slept like a baby—and you?'

'That wasn't what I meant,' she retorted, wondering what he would think if he knew she'd hardly slept at all. 'Were there any calls?'

He shook his head. 'Not until seven o'clock, then I was called to one of your patients—Seth Attrill's wife, Mabel.'

'Oh?' She frowned. 'What was wrong?'

'Her bronchial asthma was playing up—I'll enter the details on her notes then let you have them. Don't want you thinking I've been prescribing medication without informing you,' he added as he disappeared down the hall.

Irritated by his manner, Alison grabbed the coffee percolator and poured herself a mug. As if it would bother her if he saw one of her patients—he was the only one who got steamed up about things like that, and it wasn't as if she didn't tell him anyway. . . She gave a sudden guilty start. . . Paula Cotton!

In all the excitement of the previous day with Hilda she'd forgotten all about Paula Cotton. The woman's records were even now still in her case.

Clutching her mug of coffee, she made her way down the passage to her consulting-room. Early morning sunshine streamed through the high windows, flooding the room with its brightness. She paused for a moment on the threshold, her breath catching in her throat as she recalled the many times as a child she had wandered in here. Even then she had wanted to be a doctor. Even then she had been fascinated by stethoscopes, sphygmomanometers and her father's case with its tiny drawers and compartments.

She unlocked her case and took Paula Cotton's records out. Then, with the records in one hand and her coffee in the other, she crossed Reception to Grant's room.

He was sitting at his desk reading a copy of *GP News* and he looked up as Alison tapped on the door and walked straight in.

'I forgot to mention I saw Paula Cotton yesterday,' she said, coming straight to the point. She had already decided that frankness was the best form of approach but, as she plonked the records in front of him, his eyes met hers and she was unprepared for the unexpected lurch her heart gave. Her reaction must have shown on her face for they continued to stare at each other, the events of the previous evening suspended between them like some tangible thing.

Grant recovered first. 'Paula Cotton?' He glanced at the notes. 'What was the problem?'

Alison swallowed, attempted to concentrate, but was suddenly only too aware of his hands holding the magazine. Those strong, finely shaped hands that only last night had eased her tension, the same hands that years before had held her...caressed her...

'She's...she's been discharged from hospital——' she took a deep breath '—following her miscarriage...' she added, desperate to get the conversation on to a practical level.

He frowned. 'I know. I saw her the evening she was discharged after her D and C. What was the problem?'

'Depression, I would say, on the surface.'

'That's to be expected. Did they call you out for that?'

'Not entirely.' She shook her head. 'Not that I would have minded if it had only been that. It's a traumatic time for any woman.'

'Quite,' he replied, then, seeing her raised eyebrows, added, 'Hence my visit when she arrived home.'

'Yes, well, there was more to it than that.' When Grant remained silent, frowning at Paula's records, she rushed on, 'I think there's something else wrong with her.'

'Really?'

'Yes, you have to admit, it does seem strange. One

miscarriage, yes, OK, these things happen, even two maybe, but three? And then of course there are the other symptoms. . .the tiredness, the joint pains. . .'

'And the numbness in her left arm,' Grant finished for her.

'Numbness?' She paused.

'Didn't she mention that?'

'So you're aware of these things?'

'Some of them, yes. Didn't you think I would have been?' His reply was smooth, cool.

'Of course.' She coloured. 'So what's being done?'

He looked irritated, as if he resented her questioning his actions, but Alison didn't care. Paula Cotton had been a desperate woman.

'She is still in Bateman's care.'

'Bateman the gynae man?'

He nodded. 'From what I can gather, he's doing more tests. We'll see what transpires from those, then if need be I fully intend going further. Does that satisfy you?'

She nodded and suddenly felt foolish. She might have known he would be doing everything possible, bearing in mind how upset he'd been after Paula's last miscarriage.

He glanced again at the record envelope in front of him, then drew out the most recent continuation card and read her entry. 'I see you prescribed an antidepressant,' he commented at last.

'Yes.' Alison took a deep breath, preparing to defend her actions. 'I suppose you'll tell me that was wrong, that you wouldn't have done that. . .but she needed something. I thought——'

'I would have done the same,' he interrupted quietly.

She stopped in surprise and stared at him. 'You would?'

He nodded. 'There aren't too many other options at the present time, until we get the test results. . .' He paused and looked up as someone knocked at the door. 'Come in,' he called.

Gill popped her head round the door and looked quickly from one to the other of them. 'Hello,' she said. 'I wondered what was going on. Where's Hilda this morning?'

'Hilda's in hospital, Gill,' Grant replied.

'In hospital?' Gill stared at them in amazement. 'Whatever is she doing there?'

'She fell off a chair last evening,' explained Alison. 'She's broken her hip.'

'Oh, my God!' exclaimed Gill. 'Whatever's going to happen next around here?'

CHAPTER EIGHT

HILDA looked small and frail and was still drowsy from the anaesthetic when Alison visited her later that day.

'Hello, dear, what lovely flowers,' she murmured as Alison placed a bunch of freesias on the locker and sat down beside the bed.

'How are you feeling?' Alison took Hilda's hand in hers.

'A bit of a fraud really—everyone's treating me as if I'm ill.'

'It's high time you had a bit of spoiling—you've spent your life looking after others,' replied Alison firmly.

'And I'm supposed to be looking after Dr Ashton now. . .' Hilda's forehead wrinkled.

'Don't you worry about him—he's quite big enough to look after himself.'

'But there isn't much food in the house—it was nearly time for my big shop.'

'Hilda, you really must stop worrying. But if it'll make you feel better,' said Alison patiently, 'I'll go to the supermarket when I leave here and get some things I know we need.'

Hilda smiled in satisfaction and, leaning back against her pillows, closed her eyes.

She really did look very frail, Alison thought as she sat and watched her. Hilda had got old without her really noticing; it just seemed to have crept up on them.

When she guessed Hilda had dozed off Alison quietly slipped out of the ward to Sister's office.

'Hello.' Sister looked up with a smile. 'You're Alison Kennedy, aren't you? I wasn't on duty yesterday when you came in with Mrs Lloyd.'

'Hello.' Alison smiled in return. 'How is she doing?'

'Pretty good, but it was a nasty break—I think it'll take her some time to get over it. Here, take a look at her file.' She handed Alison a blue folder with Hilda's name on the outside and, as Alison opened it and was studying Hilda's post-op care plan, she added, 'It might be easier if we could stop her worrying.'

'I would say that's practically impossible.' Alison looked up from the report and gave a rueful smile. 'I've known Hilda almost all my life and she's a born worrier—I don't think we'll change her now.'

'Maybe not—she works for you, doesn't she?'

Alison nodded. 'Well, originally she worked for my father and his partner. . .'

'But you've taken your father's place now.' Sister raised her eyebrows. 'At least, according to Hilda you have—and as far as she's concerned she's looking after you and Dr Ashton.'

Alison sighed. 'It's only a temporary arrangement at the moment—nothing's been settled. . .' She trailed off as she saw the other woman's knowing grin. 'I take it you know Dr Ashton?'

'Oh, yes, we know him. Every time he comes in here he creates havoc among my nurses. . .I can't do a thing with them afterwards. . .' She trailed off as a buzzer sounded and she glanced up at the indicator board. 'Will you excuse me?' she said. 'We're a bit short-staffed today.'

'Of course.' Alison closed the folder and put it back on the desk. 'I must be going myself, but I'll just slip back and see if Hilda's awake.'

Hilda was drinking a cup of tea. She smiled at Alison over the rim of the cup. 'Hello, dear. I thought you'd gone.'

'I wouldn't go without saying goodbye. I've been talking to Sister.'

'Ah, that's better.' Hilda sighed with satisfaction. 'There's nothing like a nice cup of tea. Do you know, that's the first I've had? I couldn't drink one this morning.'

'That isn't like you, Hilda.' Alison smiled affectionately.

'I know, but I felt very queasy after my operation,' replied Hilda then, nodding across the ward, she added, 'The lady in that bed over there said she felt the same.'

Alison turned, looked at the patient opposite Hilda and saw that the card above the bed stated that her name was Ethel Blackett.

'She's just had a hip replacement,' whispered Hilda. 'She's registered with Dr Frampton but she told me just now that she's going to change to us.'

'Is that a fact?' Alison smiled. She was well used to stories of patients changing doctors.

'Yes, she said she wants a lady doctor and that a lot of her friends feel the same way.' Hilda nodded knowingly.

'In that case maybe someone should warn her that

I may not be staying,' replied Alison firmly.

'Oh, I'm sure you will now, dear.' Hilda lay back against her pillows.

'Nothing's been settled, Hilda.' Alison looked at her in mild exasperation but Hilda had closed her eyes.

With a sigh she glanced round the ward again, and as her eye caught Mrs Blackett's the other lady smiled and nodded. Alison smiled briefly back then looked quickly away. She seemed to be being drawn deeper and deeper into a way of life at Fairacre and she was still uncertain that it was what she ultimately wanted.

'You two aren't fighting, are you?' Hilda spoke suddenly, cutting into her thoughts.

Throwing her a quick glance, Alison saw that her eyes were still closed. She gave a tight little smile. 'No, Hilda,' she replied, 'we aren't fighting—at least, not so's you'd notice.'

'I do wish things could be like they used to be.' Hilda opened her eyes then and sighed wistfully.

'I know you do,' Alison laughed and stood up. 'You've said so before. But all that was a very long time ago.'

'I think Dr Ashton would like it as well.' There was a rebellious look on Hilda's face and Alison kissed her cheek, then stood looking down at her.

'I would say you're mistaken there, but he had his chance and. . .I'm not prepared to go through it all again. . .'

'Even if it wasn't his fault?'

'Hilda, that's the second time you've hinted at that,' Alison frowned. 'I think you'd better explain what you mean.'

'It's not for me to say.' Hilda's features set into a stubborn expression.

Alison gave a sigh and began to move away. 'In that case,' she said, 'I'd better be going. . .'

'One thing I will say, though,' Hilda called after her.

Alison stopped. 'What's that, Hilda?' she asked without turning round.

'It was your father in the first place that wasn't too happy about you and Dr Ashton.'

'My father?' Alison turned back to the bed. 'What do you mean, Hilda? What did my father have to do with anything?'

Hilda hesitated, then in a rush she said, 'He didn't approve when you and Dr Ashton started courting.'

Alison was forced to hide a smile at the quaintness of the old-fashioned expression. 'I'm sure you're mistaken, Hilda,' she said at last. 'My father never raised any objection to my seeing Grant Ashton.'

'Not to you maybe,' replied Hilda stubbornly, 'but he said plenty to Dr Ashton—I know, I used to hear them arguing.'

Alison stared at Hilda. 'I think you'd better tell me what you heard,' she said at last.

'I think I've said enough—you'd better ask Dr Ashton.' Hilda drew her lips into a tight line.

'Oh, come on, Hilda, you can't leave it there.' Alison was half laughing, half protesting. 'You've really got me intrigued now.'

But the mutinous expression was back on Hilda's face and she shook her head.

'Oh, well, if that's the case, and you aren't going to enlighten me any further, I might as well be off.' Alison laughed, kissed Hilda again and left the ward, only too aware as she went that Ethel Blackett was doing her best to attract her attention.

She drove straight to the supermarket but as she pushed a trolley round the store, stocking up on provisions, she found she couldn't get Hilda's comments out of her head. It was the second time she had hinted that it wasn't Grant's fault that their relationship had ended.

The first time Alison had dismissed the idea; now she was beginning to wonder. But Hilda's suggestion that it had been her father who had been in some way to blame really puzzled her. Miles Kennedy had never interfered where boyfriends had been concerned, and she certainly hadn't been aware of any objection from him towards Grant.

On her way home, as she approached the marina, on a sudden impulse she decided to call on Mabel Attrill at Marine Court, where she and Seth lived in a flat on the second floor.

Seth answered her knock. He was smoking a pipe and he took it from his mouth and stared at her in surprise.

'Well, if it isn't Dr Kennedy.' His eyes twinkled as he let her into the flat. 'Have you come to see me, Doctor?'

'No, Seth,' Alison replied, 'I've come to see your wife—how is she today?'

'She's still coughing well.' He closed the front door and led the way into the sitting-room. 'Look, Mabel,' he announced. 'Dr Kennedy's come to see you.'

Mabel, who had known Alison since she was a baby,

was sitting in a winged armchair by the window.

'Dr Kennedy?' She looked round, a startled look on her face, and peered over her glasses, then her face cleared. 'Oh, you mean Alison,' she said. 'Hello, love.' She smiled. 'How are you?'

'I'm well, Mabel,' Alison replied. 'More to the point, how are you?'

'This cough doesn't seem to get any better.' Mabel gave a deep sigh and her chest wheezed. 'But I mustn't grumble; there are plenty worse off.'

'I believe Dr Ashton came to see you?' Alison sat down and opened her case.

Mabel nodded. 'Yes, he's very nice, but I'm ever so glad you're back, Alison. I like the idea of a lady doctor.'

'I'd better have a listen to your chest now that I'm here,' said Alison quickly, not wanting to get into yet another discussion about how long she intended staying in Woodbridge.

'Very well.' Mabel sighed again. 'Go and put the kettle on, Seth,' she said to her husband who was hovering near the door.

As Seth disappeared into the kitchen Alison took her stethoscope from her case. 'Does his pipe aggravate your asthma, Mabel?' she asked quietly.

Mabel glanced at the door then nodded. 'Yes, of course it does. Always has done—but I can't expect him to give it up now, not at his time of life.'

Alison remained silent while she tested Mabel's chest, which was still very congested, then while Mabel re-buttoned her blouse she wrote up an entry in her notes.

'Dr Ashton gave me antibiotics,' said Mabel suddenly as if it had only just occurred to her to mention it. 'And he also prescribed some new spinhaler...'

'Yes, I know he did,' Alison replied without looking up, 'and I want you to finish the course of antibiotics. How are you getting on with the spinhaler?'

'Well, I must say it seems very good—so far,' replied Mabel. 'In fact it seems to be working much better than the other brand which I've used for years... Oh, no disrespect to your father, Alison,' she added hastily.

'No, of course not, Mabel. It could be that you had got too used to the old one and weren't responding to it any more. This spinhaler is new to the market and it responded very well to medical trials.'

'I'm willing to give anything a try, Alison——' Mabel sounded weary '—but I really can't ask Seth to give up his pipe.'

Alison put Mabel's records into her case, stood up, then crossed to the window. She stood for a moment looking out at the fine views down the estuary towards Yarmouth. 'I wasn't exactly suggesting that you ask Seth to give up smoking completely,' she said slowly without turning round, 'but I do think for your sake, Mabel, that we should get him to compromise.'

'What do you mean?'

Alison turned from the window and saw the dubious frown on Mabel's face.

'Well, I think we should suggest that he doesn't smoke while he's in the same room as you.'

'So where will he go? It was different when we lived in South Street—he had his allotment then, and he used to go up there for his smoke, but this is only a one-bedroomed flat, you know.'

'Yes, Mabel, I know——' Alison hesitated '—but what about the balcony?' She pointed outside the patio doors to the wrought-iron balcony that ran the length of the flat. It was bright with tubs of geraniums, busy Lizzie and lobelia. 'Maybe you could persuade Seth to take his pipe out there when he wants to smoke?' she said hopefully.

'I don't know about that.' Mabel still sounded doubtful and, as Seth came back into the room carrying a tea-tray and a plate of custard creams, she added, 'You can try if you like, Alison; perhaps it would sound better coming from you.'

'Here we are, ladies.' Seth set his tray down on to a low table then at the sudden silence glanced up. 'Was it something I said?'

'No, Seth, nothing like that.' Alison smiled. 'I was just admiring your balcony—what a lovely show of flowers you have.'

'Yes, I'm rather proud of them, even if I do say so myself.' Seth flushed with pride.

'There can't be many men who have such a nice area to sit and smoke in.'

'Eh?' He looked puzzled. 'What do you mean?'

'Well, I assumed that's where you smoke that pipe of yours,' said Alison, then added, 'I know you wouldn't smoke in here where it would aggravate Mabel's cough.'

'What?' Seth looked bewildered then, as it dawned on him what Alison was saying, he said, 'Oh, no, no, of course I wouldn't.' Then, to cover his embarrassment, he began to pour the tea.

As Alison turned back to the window she winked as she caught Mabel's eye.

Grant had started evening surgery when Alison got back to Fairacre, and as it was her evening off she set about packing the groceries away then began preparing supper.

It was while she was scrubbing new potatoes that it occurred to her that she and Grant were like an old married couple—he was at work and she was at home waiting for him and cooking his evening meal. But that, she thought with a grim little smile, was where the illusion ended. Anything less like a married couple she couldn't imagine. They couldn't seem to spend half an hour in each other's company without arguing, let alone a lifetime. There again, she thought, some married couples she knew were like that. . .

She was still smiling when Grant came into the kitchen.

'Can I share the joke?' he asked, raising his eyebrows and glancing round the room.

'Oh, it was nothing.' She shook her head, suddenly embarrassed that he should have caught her off guard.

'I've finished surgery,' he said. 'I thought I'd go down to the boat for an hour or so.' He must have seen her expression for he added, 'Don't worry, I'll take the mobile phone with me.'

'It wasn't that. . .'

'Then what?' He paused in the doorway and looked back.

'I've cooked supper.'

'You've cooked supper?' He turned again and came back into the kitchen.

'Yes, but if you've already eaten. . .'

'No, it isn't that. I was surprised, that's all.'

'Why? You cooked for me last night.'

'That's not the point. Last night was an exception. I don't expect you to cook for me because Hilda isn't here.'

She shrugged. 'It seemed the sensible thing to do. After all, I have to eat as well. Besides, Hilda was worried about you.'

He sat at the table watching her as she moved around the kitchen, serving the meal and pouring chilled Muscadet into two glasses.

'How was Hilda?' he asked after a while.

'As you would expect—but it struck me how frail she looked.'

'I'll go and see her tomorrow.'

'She'd like that.' Alison smiled. 'She seems to think the sun shines out of you.'

'I can't imagine Hilda adapting to hospital life,' he said thoughtfully, choosing to ignore her remark.

'She's not so bad as you might expect, and there's a woman in the bed opposite whom she seems to know—a Mrs Blackett.'

Grant frowned. 'Am I supposed to know her?' he asked.

'Probably not.' She gave a slight shrug. 'But according to Hilda we could be seeing more of her soon.' Grant raised his eyebrows and she went on to explain. 'She's Robert Frampton's patient apparently but she's told Hilda she'll be changing to us.'

He took a sip of wine. 'Do we know why?' He stared at her enquiringly over the rim of the glass.

'Because she prefers a female GP.' As she said it she threw him a sidelong glance, wondering what his reaction would be. When he remained silent she went on, 'And according to Hilda she isn't the only one. There is a little band of her friends out there who feel the same way.'

She expected him to be irritated, but instead he began calmly studying the contents of his glass, twisting the stem and swirling the liquid round. His reply when it came surprised her.

'That merely confirms what I'd always suspected,' he said.

'Which is?'

'That female GPs are an asset to any practice—they attract business.'

'Was that why you agreed to give this arrangement a try?'

Again she expected him to be annoyed and was further surprised when he threw back his head and laughed. 'Oh, come on, Alison, you know me better than that.'

She shrugged and turned back to the oven, opening the door and lifting out the vegetable dishes that she'd put in to warm.

He watched her for a moment, then said, 'So what's Hilda going to say to her new friend?'

'Goodness knows. I reminded her that nothing was settled yet.'

He sat down at the table, folded his arms and leaned back in his chair, tilting it on to two legs.

'Of course,' he mused as he watched her set the dishes on the table, 'even though nothing is settled, we can't let things stand still where the practice is concerned, otherwise it will go downhill and we'll start losing patients instead of attracting them.'

'You mean we should allow people to think that I am here permanently?' She stared at him as he began helping himself to vegetables.

'It might not be a bad thing. I can't afford to let things slide too much, Alison. I have my future to consider as well, and as I said before I have plans—lots of plans.'

She picked up her knife and fork. 'You obviously don't intend wasting any time... My father's only been gone——'

'Alison!' he interrupted her in mid-sentence, setting his knife and fork down and staring at her across the table. 'Your father knew of these plans—he'd approved them. Oh, he wasn't too keen on all of them, that's true, especially the thought of computerisation, but he saw the necessity for them, knew it was the way forward—"something for the next generation", was the way he put it.'

'So when do you intend putting these plans into operation?' Her tone was cool.

'I think that rather depends on you.'

'Me?' She raised her eyebrows.

'Yes, and on whether or not you intend staying. I can hardly instigate things on my own—I would need to know what your plans are for the future before I could proceed any further.'

'We said six months' trial...' she began warily.

He nodded. 'I know, and I intend to honour that agreement, but I think you should be aware of the facts.'

She was silent for a moment, pushing a piece of fish around her plate, then, glancing up at him again, she said, 'Would you say there's a danger of any patients leaving the practice if they were aware of the present situation?'

'Could be.' He shrugged.

'But people in Woodbridge have been with this practice all their lives. . .' she began, thinking he was being unnecessarily alarmist.

'Alison——' he set down his knife and fork again and stared at her in mild exasperation '——you know as well as I do that people don't like change; it unsettles them.'

'Even so——' she protested.

'They were loyal to your father,' he went on, not giving her a chance to say more, 'and I believe his patients would transfer their loyalties to you, but the public are fickle, and if there is something that people like even less than change it's uncertainty.' He shrugged again. 'All I'm saying is we can't afford to hang around for too long. We need to get our act together. It's an unfortunate fact of life, Alison, but these days general practice is a business and any business has to be competitive or it goes under.'

'So what, in your opinion, needs to be done?' Coolly she surveyed him across the table. 'What are these plans you were talking about?'

'We need,' he replied firmly, 'to expand—a larger practice, with preferably three partners, two nursing sisters to run extra clinics, complete computerisation and ancillary staff to deal with administration—a practice manager, a secretary and at least three receptionists.'

She stared at him incredulously. 'Are you joking?'

'No, Alison,' he replied smoothly, 'I'm deadly serious.'

'And how do you propose we'd fit all that in here at Fairacre?'

'We either get planning permission—there's plenty of room at the side of the house for another extension —or, failing that, we find a plot of land and build a new centre.'

'And how do you think we would pay for it all?' There was a scathing note in her voice.

'We would qualify for government help,' he replied firmly.

She stared at him for a long moment. 'I wonder what my father's reaction would have been to all that,' she remarked drily at last.

'Part of it was at his suggestion,' he replied and, as he saw her look of surprise, he added, 'The further extension to Fairacre, as a matter of fact.'

Alison pushed her chair back and stood up. 'You appear to have it all worked out,' she said abruptly.

'Sort of.'

'I'm sorry, Grant——' she looked down at him '—but we agreed on six months and I don't intend to allow you to rush me.'

He shrugged. 'I wouldn't dream of it.' He was interrupted by the ringing of the telephone on the dresser behind him and he leaned back to answer it.

As he spoke to the person on the other end of the line Alison's mind was racing. In spite of the misgivings she still had about the practicalities of her and Grant's working together permanently, the plans he had outlined for the future of the practice had excited her—they presented a challenge, a professional challenge she suddenly longed to be a part of. And at the same time she knew she couldn't bear it if the Fairacre practice was to go under. She owed it to her father never to let that happen. She had agreed to the six-month trial out of love for her father and deference to his wishes, but from the start she'd had her doubts about a long-term commitment. Already there had been friction and coolness between herself and Grant, and constantly there was the reminder of the way things had once been, and then of the way he had treated her.

A sudden thought hit her and she looked up sharply.

'Grant. . .' she began as he replaced the receiver.

'Yes?' He stood up.

She glanced at the phone. 'Do you have to go out?'

He nodded. 'Yes, a home confinement. The midwife wants me there—it's a difficult breech delivery.'

'Oh, I see.'

He paused and looked down at her. 'Were you going to say something?'

She hesitated. Now was not the right time to question him about Hilda's theories. 'No, nothing—you go, I'll tidy up here.'

'OK.' He walked to the door then stopped and looked back. 'Oh, Alison.'

118   STRICTLY PROFESSIONAL

'Yes?' She looked up and at the sudden look of tender amusement in his eyes felt her heart skip a beat. 'Thanks for the supper,' he said softly.

CHAPTER NINE

ALMOST without their realising it Alison and Grant slipped into a routine, and during the next week while Hilda remained in hospital they took it in turns to visit her, to do the shopping and to cook meals. Grant said nothing further about his plans for the practice and Alison decided that she wouldn't be hurried into making premature decisions.

Ken Bridges, the manager of the marina, came to one early morning surgery.

'Your back's no better, then, Ken?' Alison looked up sympathetically as he walked gingerly into her room and sat down.

'No, afraid not.' He grimaced. 'I've tried rest and pain-killers but they haven't worked this time.'

'Well, let's have a look at you.' Alison stood up. 'Do you think you could get on to the couch?'

Ken stood up again and pulled a face. 'I'll have a go,' he said, then walked slowly across the room and eased himself on to her examination couch.

Gently Alison tested the elevation of his legs then, starting with the vertebrae in his neck, she examined the length of his spine.

'I think,' she said at last, straightening up, 'the best thing would be for me to make an appointment for you to have some physiotherapy.'

'Er. . .yes, all right.' Ken sounded doubtful and

Alison, who had been about to walk back to her desk, paused and looked down at him.

'You sound dubious, Ken. Are you not keen on that idea?'

'Oh, no, it's nothing like that, Alison,' he replied hastily. 'It's just that, I was wondering. . .'

'Yes, go on.'

'Whether I could see Dr Ashton.'

'Dr Ashton?' She paused. 'Why?'

'Well, in the past whenever I've had trouble with my back, if the rest and pain-killers didn't work, your father used to get Dr Ashton to do a spot of massage and manipulation on me. . .and to be honest that put me right long before I could get an appointment for physiotherapy. He's very good, you know, Dr Ashton, at the old massage,' he added a trifle anxiously when Alison didn't immediately answer.

I don't doubt it, she thought as she walked back to her desk; she remembered only too well the times, one so very recently, when his hands had massaged and eased away her own tension.

'So would you mind?' Ken, still on the couch, turned his head to look at her.

'Mind? Why should I mind?'

'I don't know.' Ken hesitated. 'I thought you doctors sometimes got a bit edgy about seeing each other's patients. . .'

'I don't know where you got that idea, Ken.'

'So you'll ask him for me?'

'I'll do better than that—I'll go now and see if he's finished surgery.'

Leaving Ken lying on the couch, Alison strode out

of her consulting-room and into Reception where she found Grant talking to Gill.

He looked up as she approached.

'Grant——' she swallowed '—would you look at a patient for me?'

'Are you asking for a second opinion?'

She tried to ignore the amusement in his eyes. 'Not really. The patient suffers from a bulging disc and I wondered if you'd give him some manipulation.'

'Of course.' All traces of amusement were gone now and he followed her back to her room.

'Hello, Ken!' As Alison shut the door behind them, Grant crossed to the couch. 'I didn't know it was you.'

'Hello, Grant.' Ken turned his head sideways and gave a rueful grin. 'I hope it doesn't make a difference.'

'Of course not.' Grant smiled at Alison. 'Ken and I are old friends.'

'I gathered that,' she replied, then stood back and watched as Grant slipped off his jacket and turned back his shirt-cuffs.

'How long has it been like this, Ken?' he asked a moment later.

'About a week—I've tried the usual rest and painkiller routine but it hasn't worked.'

'Right, let's have a look at you, then.' Grant leaned over the couch and began to examine Ken as Alison had done.

As the strong, finely shaped hands moved over the man's back Alison watched, remembering again how those same hands had moved down her own spine, easing stress, healing. . .and as the massage intensified she became mesmerised, recalling other, more distant occasions when those hands had held her, caressed her, loved her...

She mustn't think of that now.

Desperately she turned away and stared out of the window. Would she ever forget? Could she really work alongside this man forever and pretend nothing had happened between them?

At long last Grant straightened up and moved back from the couch. 'I hope that will bring you some relief, Ken,' he said. 'If it doesn't, come back and see Alison and we'll arrange another session. For the time being, though, I suggest you go home, take some more pain-killers and get some rest.'

'Yes, of course.' Ken eased himself into a sitting position. 'Thanks a lot, Grant. That feels better already.'

With a nod to Alison, Grant crossed to the door.

'Thank you, Grant.' Quietly Alison echoed Ken's gratitude with her own.

As the door closed Ken said, 'I've run out of pain-killers, Alison.'

'I'll write you a prescription.' She sat down at her desk and pulled a prescription pad towards her.

'Will you be staying at Fairacre now, Alison?' asked Ken a few minutes later as he cautiously eased himself into his jacket.

'Nothing's really been decided yet,' she replied without looking up.

'I'd have thought it's an ideal little set-up,' he said thoughtfully. 'You're an islander, Alison, one of us— there aren't too many left, you know.'

'I know, Ken.' She laughed. 'I'd noticed.'

'So we can't afford to lose anyone.' He straightened his tie and, taking the prescription she handed him, stared at it for a moment. 'Grant was telling me recently that he was keen to install a computer system here,' he added. 'I showed him our system at the marina actually—he seemed very interested.'

Alison pulled a face. 'Can't say computers are my strong point, I'm afraid.'

'Ah, thing of the future. We won't be able to exist without them soon—but you shouldn't be afraid; they're easy once you get the hang of them. Take Cheryl for example—she wasn't keen to learn but now she uses them all the time, and quite honestly——' he lowered his voice and glanced over his shoulder '—if Cheryl can get the hang of them anyone can.'

'Thanks, Ken,' Alison replied drily, then smiled as he realised what he had implied and reddened slightly.

'Oh, I'm sorry,' he said hastily. 'I didn't mean. . .'

'No, Ken, I know you didn't,' she laughed.

He glanced at his prescription again. 'Seriously, though, Alison, you wouldn't have to hand-write all these if you had a computer. Tell you what, why don't you pop into the marina when you're passing and Cheryl can show you our system?'

'Thanks.' She followed him to the door. 'That's kind of you.'

'No problem; I'll tell Cheryl to look out for you.'

No doubt she'll be enthralled, Alison thought wryly as she closed the door behind Ken. He quite obviously was unaware that she and Cheryl had never been bosom pals.

She sat down at her desk again and flicked the intercom. 'Anyone else for me, Gill?' she asked.

'No, Alison, that's the lot for the moment.'

'What are the visits like?'

'Rather a lot, I'm afraid.'

'OK—a quick coffee then I'll get started. I must get to the shops—it's my turn to cook tonight.'

'I don't know why you don't get someone else in while Hilda's away,' replied Gill. 'It would make life so much easier for you and Dr Ashton when you are both so busy.'

Maybe it would make life easier, she thought as she flicked the switch back, but it wouldn't be so much fun. It had become quite a test of their culinary skills to produce dinner every evening, with each of them trying to outdo the other.

She was about to leave her room when the intercom sounded and Gill informed her that a Mrs Dawson was asking to see her.

'Mrs Brenda Dawson?'

'Yes, that's right, Alison,' Gill replied, 'and, before you say it, yes, I know she's Dr Ashton's patient.'

'Does she have an appointment, Gill?' asked Alison.

'No, she says she doesn't want an appointment, simply that she happened to be passing and she just wants a quick word—I've pointed out that if everyone did that there'd be no time for you to do anything else in the course of a day, but I'm sorry, she's insisting that I ask you if you'll spare her a minute.'

'All right, Gill, ask her to come in.' With a sigh Alison sat down again, wondering how she was going to get round this situation.

'Hello, Dr Kennedy.' Brenda Dawson came into the room and stood by the door.

'Hello, Mrs Dawson, won't you take a seat?' Alison indicated the chair alongside her desk.

The woman shook her head. 'No, I won't take up more than a moment of your time; you see, I just wanted to thank you.'

'To thank me?' Alison frowned.

'Yes, for having a word with Dr Ashton.'

'You made an appointment. . .?'

'I didn't need to. Thanks to you, he called to see me. . . He said you'd told him of the problems I've been having. We talked everything through and you were right, he was really kind; it was like he really understood what I'd been going through. He prescribed HRT for me. I have to use patches that stick on my skin so that the hormones are absorbed into my bloodstream. He said I should begin to feel better quite soon and that he would keep close checks on my blood-pressure and carry out regular cervical smears and breast examinations.'

She paused for breath. 'And do you know,' she continued, 'he even explained it all to my husband? Even Alan's in favour of HRT now, since Dr Ashton told him that it helps prevent brittle bones and heart disease. Anyway, Dr Kennedy, I won't take up more of your time. I just wanted you to know, that's all. . .I hope you didn't mind my coming in.'

'Not at all, Mrs Dawson.' Alison smiled. 'I'm pleased that you did and I'm even more pleased that Dr Ashton was able to help you.'

As Brenda Dawson left the surgery Alison felt a

sense of satisfaction creep over her, satisfaction that she and Grant seemed to have acted as a team.

Her house calls for that day were scattered over the area, a terminally ill cancer patient in one part of the town who needed her morphine dose increased, a child with mumps in another, a baby from one of the outlying farms suffering from croup, and a man on one of the houseboats moored at the mouth of the estuary who needed antibiotics for chronic bronchitis.

She completed the list by lunchtime and decided to collect her shopping from the supermarket before going home.

She was cooking lemon chicken that evening, and she collected the ingredients and was just leaving the checkout when she almost collided with Paula Cotton who was on her way into the store.

'Paula! Hello!'

'Hello, Dr Kennedy.'

'How are you?' Alison looked closely at Paula, noticing her high colour and the look of fatigue in her eyes.

'Not much better.' She shook her head.

'Oh, Paula, I'm sorry to hear that.' Alison stared at her in concern. 'Have you seen Dr Ashton again?'

'Yes, I came in yesterday. He phoned me to say he'd had some of my test results from the hospital.'

'And?'

'They don't seem to be any the wiser.' Paula helplessly shook her head. 'He's going to arrange for me to see someone else.'

'Well, try not to worry too much.' Alison hoped she sounded reassuring. 'I'm sure they'll sort something out in time.' She watched as Paula walked on into the store and found herself struggling with something that was niggling at the back of her mind, something elusive, something to do with Paula's condition.

She took the coast road back to Fairacre, driving slowly, enjoying the scenery and listening to a local station on the car radio. The tide was out, a distant line sparkling on the horizon, while inshore black-headed gulls swooped over the mouth of the estuary pecking at the exposed weed-covered bed. A group of children ran with a black dog over the mudflats, their voices shrill in the quiet afternoon air.

The radio presenter announced a request for a lady living in Newport and, as the strains of a well-known aria filled the car, it reminded Alison of a concert she had attended during her training. At the thought of Crandelbury Street, the elusive factor that had been niggling at the back of her mind since seeing Paula Cotton suddenly clicked into place.

When she reached Fairacre she went straight to her consulting-room and, picking up the telephone receiver, dialled the Crandelbury Street number.

On the fourth ring, Helen, one of the receptionists, answered, giving the familiar practice number.

'Hello, Helen? It's Alison Kennedy.'

'Oh, Dr Kennedy. How nice to hear from you. How are you?'

'Very well, Helen—is Dr Richards there?'

'Yes, I'll just put you through.'

'Alison!' Seconds later she heard the senior partner's voice.

'Hello, Diana.'

'How are you? How are things going?'

'Very well, surprisingly.' She laughed.

'I told you they would. So you're not ringing to beg me to take you back?'

'Not quite! No, actually, Diana, I need some information. My training files are in a case in the library cupboard—do you think you could find the red file marked "SLE" and put it in the post to me?'

'Yes, of course. I'll go and do it now.' Diana paused. 'Do you think you've got a similar case?'

'I'm not sure—but I think it could be. I want to check that file before I make a fool of myself.'

'Very well, I'll put it in the post.'

'Thanks, Diana.' She paused. 'Say hello to everyone for me, won't you?'

'Of course—we were only talking about you yesterday and wondering how you were getting on, and whether you were missing us all.'

She didn't know what else to say. Was she missing them? Her friends? Her job? If she was honest, the Crandelbury Street practice seemed a million miles away.

Thoughtfully, with a promise to Diana that she would ring again, she hung up and sat for a moment staring at the phone, then with a shrug she stood up and made her way to the kitchen to start preparing dinner.

The following day was so busy that it was not until late evening that Alison had time to read the file that had arrived for her in the second post. Grant had cooked supper for them both, then had gone out to visit a patient who needed a nebuliser for a severe asthma attack.

The house was quiet and, taking the file with her to the bathroom, Alison ran herself a bath, pouring in a generous supply of aromatic oils, intending to pamper herself for a change.

After coiling her long hair and pinning it on top of her head into a loose knot, she undressed and stepped into the bath. For a long while she simply relaxed, luxuriating in the scented water, allowing the stresses of the day to float away, then, taking the file from the chair beside the bath, she opened it and began to read.

She became so absorbed by what she was reading that she lost all track of time and it was the distant click of the front door that finally roused her, and she looked up with a start.

The water had grown quite cool and with a grimace she stood up, reached for a towel and stepped out of the bath. Quickly she dried herself then paused and listened and, hearing Grant talking on the phone, she grabbed her bathrobe and pulled it on. Tying the robe tightly around her, she hurried on to the landing and looked over the banisters.

Grant was sitting on the stairs talking into his mobile phone. He had removed his jacket, loosened his tie and turned back the cuffs of his shirt. His dark hair was tousled and, as usual, fell over his forehead.

He glanced up and saw her and there was something in his expression that made her grip the banister rail more tightly. Without taking his eyes from her face he said goodbye to whoever he had been talking to and replaced the phone aerial.

'Is there anything wrong?' He stood up and stared quizzically at her.

'No, nothing,' she said quickly. 'I wanted to catch you, that's all.'

'Really?'

'I was afraid you might be going out again.'

There was a gleam of amusement in his green eyes. 'I was thinking about it,' he said, then added softly, 'But if you have something else in mind. . .' His gaze flickered from her face to her bathrobe, then to her hair, tendrils of which she could feel had escaped from the knot and were lying damply against her neck and shoulders.

She stared down at him for a moment, then she felt the colour flood her cheeks as she realised how it must look to him.

'I. . . I. . . I've been doing some reading, about a case. . .I simply wanted to tell you what I'd found out. . .' He had begun to climb the stairs and she trailed off in confusion.

'Now, isn't that a shame?' he said softly. 'Just for one moment there I was thinking that maybe it was me you wanted, when all the time it was work you wanted to discuss—just like it always is these days, eh, Alison?'

By this time he had reached her on the landing and involuntarily she backed away, wary now of the look in his eyes—a look she had seen before—a look she remembered only too well.

'But it wasn't always like that, was it?' He was standing in front of her, had trapped her against the banisters. 'I can remember a time when work was the last thing on our minds. . .'

'Grant,' she began warningly, 'we agreed. . .a professional relationship. . .'

'Oh, yes, I forgot. . .a professional relationship. . . but do you know something? I've had enough of that, Alison,' he said softly. 'I've had enough of us working together, living together, eating together but not being able to do anything else together.' He put his hands either side of her on the banisters, imprisoning her, and she stiffened as she caught the familiar scent of him.

'Oh, it might have worked,' he went on relentlessly in the same soft tones, 'if I hadn't known anything else, if we were simply strangers, colleagues, but we aren't, are we?'

'What do you mean?' Helplessly she stared at him.

'What do I mean?' he repeated, allowing his gaze to roam over her face, her hair, the open neck of her bathrobe where the tops of her breasts were just visible. 'You forget, I've known what it's like to make love to you—to have you love me, so as far as I'm concerned I don't give a damn any more for keeping things professional.'

As he was speaking he pulled her roughly into his arms and as she opened her mouth to protest he brought his own mouth down on to hers, silencing her with an angry, passionate kiss.

'Have you any idea what it's been like,' he demanded, tearing himself away at last, leaving her breathless, 'being here alone in the house with you—

every night—wanting you, but not daring to touch—have you any idea at all?'

'But. . .we agreed. . .'

'To hell with what we agreed! Why do you think I was sleeping on the boat?'

'I thought. . .'

'It was to get out of temptation's way, that's why! There were times when it was unbearable knowing you were here in the house. . .in the next bedroom. . . There were times, lady, I'll have you know, when you were in grave danger of being ravished in your bed! Times when I knew if I stayed I wouldn't be able to keep my hands off you.'

'Grant. . . I. . .'

Again he silenced her, stifling her protest with another kiss, parting her lips, entangling his fingers in her hair. Still she struggled, wanting him, but furious with herself for doing so.

Then, as his arms went around her, gradually the wanting outweighed the fury, and in spite of everything she felt herself slowly begin to respond to his touch as her body came alive.

Long-forgotten desires struggled to the surface as they relived in vivid detail those exciting moments of their past. Helplessly she allowed her arms to creep around his neck, her fingers to sink into the dark hair as his hands moved urgently over her body, moulding breasts and hips, untying her robe, parting the material, allowing the garment to slip to the floor.

She could do nothing to stop him when he lowered his head and cupped one breast, taking the nipple into his mouth; was powerless when he half carried her to his bedroom and lowered her on to his bed; didn't want to stop him when he undressed, discarding his own clothes in a frenzy of desire, and welcomed him with a gasp of delight as their flesh merged.

And suddenly, as the barriers dissolved and they rose and fell to the rhythm of their love, it was as if they'd never been apart.

Wordlessly they clung to each other, helpless in the overwhelming intensity of their reunion.

'Alison. . .!' At the peak of his passion he called her name and, as she held him against her, her cheeks were wet with tears.

Much later, as they lay in a tangle of sheets and the room grew dark around them, he threw his arms wide.

'I always knew you'd come back to me some day,' he said softly.

CHAPTER TEN

'I WOULD say, Dr Ashton, that was a pretty arrogant assumption.'

'No, not arrogant—simply inevitable.'

'Well, I'd call it arrogant,' she retorted, 'especially after the way you treated me.' Her body still throbbed, still glowed with fulfilment, but already she was beginning to wonder what she'd done.

'The way I treated you! What about the way you've treated me?' he protested.

'What do you mean?' Lifting herself on to one elbow and staring indignantly down at him, she was just able to make out the line of his profile in the half-light.

'What do I mean? How about avoiding me?'

'Avoiding you?' She frowned, knowing what he meant but playing for time.

'Yes, avoiding me. Come on, Ali, when you came home it was when you knew I wasn't going to be here——'

'Can you blame me for that?' she exclaimed. 'After what happened? You used me, Grant!'

'No, Alison!' His voice was like a whiplash, then more quietly he said, 'No, never that.'

'Then what?' She frowned, bewildered by what he was saying, then suddenly she remembered something else. 'I want to know, Grant. Even Hilda keeps hinting there was more to what happened between us than met the eye. I didn't know what she was talking about—I thought she was suffering from the after-effects of the anaesthetic.'

He had grown very still. 'What did she say?' he asked quietly at last.

'She tried to tell me that my father had something to do with our splitting up.'

'And did you believe her?'

'Of course I didn't!' she retorted. 'That's nonsense. My father was never that strict. He was always easy-going where boyfriends were concerned.'

'Ah, but in my case it was a bit different.' His tone when he answered was quiet and there was an edge to it she didn't recognise.

'What do you mean?' she demanded.

'Think about it, Alison,' he said softly. 'Think about what was happening in your life when I first came to Woodbridge.'

'I don't understand,' she replied, shaking her head.

He leaned across the bed and switched on the bedside light. The room became suffused with a soft, amber glow and instinctively Alison pulled the sheet up to cover her breasts.

He turned and looked at her. 'You seem to have forgotten that when you and I met we struck sparks off each other.'

She made a sharp, dismissive little gesture.

'Well, we did, didn't we?' He gave a cryptic smile. 'It was instantaneous, if I remember rightly—the air crackled. Anyway, your father was very aware of it. . .'

'He never said anything,' said Alison slowly, trying hard to remember.

'He thought it best to leave well alone; that it all might die a natural death when you went back to medical school——'

She looked up quickly and met his gaze but what she saw there made her look away again.

'But, as we know, it didn't,' he said softly. 'You could have said the old saying of absence making the heart grow fonder had been invented purely for us.' Reaching out his hand, he took a strand of her hair and began to wind it round his fingers. 'I seem to recall you coming back to the island every spare moment you had——'

'That's quite true,' she interrupted him sharply, not wanting him to go into further detail, unwilling, even after what had just happened, to recall the desperate longing she had felt at that time, 'but I still don't remember my father making any objection.'

'He didn't,' Grant said softly, then added, 'At least not to you.'

'You mean he did to you?' She stared at him, recalling Hilda's words.

He shrugged. 'He was very subtle at first; he merely reminded me how young you were—too young to know your own mind, was how he put it—and that you were on the brink of your career. Then, as time went on, he seemed to get annoyed at the number of times you came home.'

'Go on,' she said faintly, wondering what on earth she was going to hear next.

'The crunch came when you had severe problems with that set of exams—remember?'

'Only too well.' She shuddered. 'But you helped me

with the revision for the retakes. . .'

'I seem to remember most of the revision took place in the cabin of *The Kittihawk*. . .'

She coloured. 'So what happened after that?' she asked quickly, ignoring the amusement in his eyes.

'Your father stopped pussy-footing around and gave it to me straight—cool it with you and let you get on with your career.'

'So what was your reaction to that?'

'I told him I was in love with you.'

She stared at him and felt her heart twist.

'His answer was that, if that was the case, then I should be prepared to stand back and let you achieve your lifelong ambition. He said that I knew as well as he did the amount of commitment that was needed for a medical training and that you weren't adapting yourself to it while you were constantly coming home to see me.'

As Grant finished speaking Alison sat up and leaned forward. 'It would have been nice if someone had asked me what I wanted,' she said bitterly.

'And what would you have said?' asked Grant.

She felt her hands tighten into fists and she turned her head away.

'It wasn't what I wanted, Alison,' he said quietly.

'Then why did you go along with it?' she demanded, rounding sharply on him.

'I realised your father was right and I thought it would only be for a while—that when you got yourself through the bulk of your training I could get things back the way they were.'

'But you never even attempted that!' she retorted accusingly.

'I underestimated the intensity of your reactions, then later I wondered if your father had been right and that you really had been too young to know your own mind.'

'What do you mean?' she demanded. 'What gives you the right to think that?'

'Well, you replaced me pretty quickly, didn't you?' He raised his arms behind his head, leaning back against the headboard.

'Replaced you?' She stared at him in growing bewilderment. 'What on earth are you talking about?'

'I came up to London—to your college.'

She frowned. 'You came up several times. . .'

'I know, but this time was after we'd split up.'

'What do you mean? I don't remember. . .'

'Of course you don't—you didn't see me; you were too wrapped up in your new boyfriend.'

'Grant——' she stared at him in exasperation '—I haven't got a clue what you're talking about.'

'I suppose you're going to tell me next that you haven't heard of Simon Faulkener.'

'Simon. . .! Oh!' Her hand flew to her mouth.

'I see that rings a bell with you,' he said wryly.

'But. . .but. . .I don't understand. Simon and I. . . we. . .we only. . .' She trailed off. 'But how did you. . .?'

'How did I know about him? I'll tell you how I know, Alison. As I said, I came up to London—I know I'd promised your father I'd leave you alone, but the truth was I couldn't bear it any longer. I had to see if you were all right. When I arrived at the college one of the students told me you had gone out with this Simon Faulkener character. I'm not ashamed to admit I asked a few questions, and it seemed as though you and he had a relationship going. Anyway, I hung around and saw the pair of you come back... From what I saw I gathered you'd got over me pretty quickly.'

'You'd hurt me, Grant! Hurt me more than I'd ever been hurt before...'

'Well, you got your own back, Alison, I can assure you—because do you know something? I was jealous...jealous of that schoolboy you were with.'

'Simon wasn't a schoolboy...' she protested.

'He was still wet behind the ears!'

'I'll have you know Simon was very nice...'

'Oh, I'm sure he was.' He laughed. 'But I bet you didn't have as good a time with him as you did with me——'

'How dare you——?' She lifted her hand as if to hit him, but he laughingly caught her wrist and held it, then abruptly he let her go and in the same movement reached out and, grasping the back of her neck, forced her head down and covered her lips with his mouth in a hard, almost brutal kiss.

'I thought you didn't care,' she muttered when just as abruptly he released her. 'I thought you'd used me. I went out with Simon, and a couple of others,' she added, 'purely to try to forget you.'

'And did it work?' There was a mocking expression now in his green eyes.

'What do you think...?' she whispered.

They stared at each other for a long moment, then Grant sighed. 'At least your father got his wish and saw you qualify.'

'Why didn't you tell me about all this before?'

'Your father asked me not to; he knew that if you thought he was interfering you would have rebelled—you were pretty headstrong in those days. . .' He grinned and she punched his arm in protest.

'The thing was,' he went on quietly after a while, 'as Miles and I got to know each other better we became friends as well as partners. I was angry with him at first for trying to come between us, but as time went on I saw that he'd been right—that if we'd gone on as we were you would have blown your career.'

'But he knew our relationship had ended; he must have realised how difficult a partnership would be between us now. . .'

'Maybe once you were qualified he simply wanted you to carry on the Kennedy tradition at Fairacre.'

'I still wish he'd come to me about it,' said Alison tightly.

'But would you have been prepared to listen, to compromise?'

'I doubt it.' She pulled a face. 'I dare say I thought I knew best.'

'You certainly wouldn't have thanked your father for interfering.'

'I'm not certain I can forgive him for that even now,' she replied grimly.

'You mean I was the love of your life?'

'I didn't say that. . .'

'And that no man has matched up since?'

'You are quite insufferable, Grant Ashton,' she replied lightly, wondering at the same time what his reaction would be if he knew he spoke the truth.

They fell silent, each reflecting on what might have been. In the end it was Grant who asked the inevitable question.

'So where do we go from here?' he said softly.

Slowly she shook her head. 'I don't know.'

'I think we should look at the facts. . .'

'Which are?'

He paused, reflecting. 'There was an instant attraction between us,' he said at last, 'and we loved each other; that love was put on hold; maybe we've been given a second chance. . .'

'We can't just pick up where we left off. . .' she protested.

'Of course not.' He looked suitably shocked. 'But. . .'

'But what?'

'It's still good between us. . .isn't it? Alison?' he prompted and, when she remained silent, he added, 'Or maybe you didn't think it was good. . .'

She turned and looked at him then. 'You know damn well it was good.'

'So. . .?' He reached out and began playing with her hair again. 'Shall we give it another try?'

Still she hesitated. 'I don't know, Grant,' she said at last.

He shrugged. 'OK. So we take things slowly? See what develops?'

'I'm not sure. . .' She shook her head. She was too vulnerable. . .the wound still hurt. Only now it was different. Now he was saying he had loved her. He hadn't used her. He'd even come to find her. . . Part of her longed to say yes, that she still loved him. After all, he had explained now. . . Maybe. . .maybe. . .

'We'll give ourselves time and see what happens,' he said, then gently he tugged at her hair, pulling her head back. 'But in the meantime how about we make up for a little more lost time?'

She opened her mouth to protest. . .to say she had things to do. . .to say she really mustn't stay. . .but even before she could form the words he moved in behind her, his body warm against her back, his hands cupping her breasts as he began kissing the hollow of her neck.

Weakly she leaned against him as for the second time that night her body came alive to his touch.

The following morning Alison imagined that the fact that she and Grant had spent the night together was somehow emblazoned on her forehead in foot-high letters for all the world to see. When, to her surprise, Gill behaved quite normally, grumbling about the post being late and that a vase of tulips in the hall had shed their petals all over the carpet, Alison didn't know whether she felt relieved or disappointed.

Taking her surgery notes and a mug of coffee with her, she shut herself in her consulting-room away from Grant's faintly amused demeanour.

Already, in spite of the fact that their lovemaking had been every bit as wonderful as she had remembered it to be, she was beginning to regret what had happened between them. How could she possibly maintain a strictly professional relationship with him now, after the night they had just spent?

On the other hand, in spite of his explanations, she still wasn't certain that she could trust either him or herself again. She had been too hurt and it had taken her too long to get over it for her to hurtle headlong into another relationship with him.

Someone tapped on her door, breaking into her thoughts, and she looked up sharply. Before she even had a chance to answer, Grant stuck his head round the door.

'I was just wondering. . .' he said.

'Yes?' She raised her eyebrows.

'You had something to tell me.'

'I did?' She frowned.

'Yes, when you flew out of the bathroom last night and attempted to seduce me——'

'Grant. . .' she began warningly.

'Sorry.' He lifted his arms as if to fend her off. 'Sorry. But seriously——' he came right into the room, closing the door behind him, and perched on the edge of her desk '—you were excited about something—I would like to think that it was purely due to the fact that I had come home, but I have a feeling there was rather more to it than that.' The green eyes gleamed wickedly and she was forced to laugh.

'Yes, there was rather more to it than that,' she agreed, and when he pulled a face she went on quickly, 'It was about one of your patients in actual fact.'

'I see—another take-over.'

'What do you mean?' She stared at him.

'Another case like Brenda Dawson that you think I've got wrong... Well, come on, let's have it—who is it this time?'

'Grant, I never said you were wrong about Brenda Dawson. I merely thought——'

'I know. It's OK, Alison, really it is—I just like to see your eyes flash when you get angry with me.'

'Oh!'

'And your cheeks change to that glorious colour...'

'Grant, I'm going to throw you out of my surgery in a moment...'

'No, don't do that. I want to know. Really I do.' He looked serious.

'Well——' she remained doubtful, unconvinced that he wasn't merely teasing her '—actually it was Paula Cotton.'

'Paula? Now why did I have the feeling it might be something to do with her?' He paused, smiled, then went on, 'Come on, then, let's have it—what do you think is wrong with Paula—apart from the fact that she can't carry a baby full-term?'

Alison took a deep breath. 'I think she might be suffering from SLE,' she replied quietly.

He stared at her for a long moment without speaking, and her heart sank as she thought he was thinking her suggestion ridiculous.

Then very slowly he said, 'SLE?'

'Yes,' she nodded. 'Systemic lupus——'

'Erythematosus,' he finished for her. 'Yes, I know what it means.' He slid from the edge of the desk, walked to the window and with his back to her stood looking out.

Anxiously Alison watched him, wondering if he would simply dismiss her theory.

At last he said, 'It's fairly rare, you know.'

'It's as common as multiple sclerosis or leukaemia in this country,' she replied stoutly, poised to defend herself. 'But hardly anyone seems to have heard of it,' she added.

'Have you come across it before?' he turned and looked at her curiously.

'Yes.' She nodded. 'There was a patient in Crandelbury Street—I studied her case history as part of my training.'

'So what makes you think it may be Paula's problem?' he asked quietly.

She swallowed, still unsure of his reaction. 'It wasn't until I met Paula yesterday, coming into the supermarket, that I became suspicious—she had a very high colour across her cheeks.'

He frowned. 'I haven't noticed that.'

'It isn't there all the time,' she replied quickly. 'It's known as the wolf mask—hence the name lupus,' she explained. She threw him a quick glance, uncertain whether he had known that or not, then she went on hurriedly, not giving him chance to comment, 'She had it when I visited her at home...but I didn't think anything of it then. And there are other things, of course...'

'Go on.' He looked interested now.

'Well——' she took a deep breath, '—as you know, she has suffered from aching joints and the weakness in her arm and hand. SLE is apparently know as the Great Impersonator because it mimics other conditions and is so difficult to diagnose—her attacks seem to be triggered by her pregnancies.'

He frowned again. 'I can't see why that——'

'The patient I studied was just the same,' Alison broke in eagerly. 'In her case she had suffered six miscarriages and had gone undiagnosed for years.'

'Six miscarriages!' He stared at her. 'Good God!'

'Yes. Before she was finally diagnosed she suffered hypertension and mitral heart disease which steadily worsened. It wasn't until she began experiencing epileptic fits that the diagnosis was reached.'

He continued to stare at her. 'And you think this is what is wrong with Paula Cotton.' It was a statement rather than a question, and abruptly he turned back to the window.

'Grant,' she began hesitantly, 'I'm sorry, I didn't mean to interfere. It's just that in the other patient's case—the woman at Crandelbury Street—her condition went on for so long undiagnosed and she seemed to suffer so much unnecessarily. . .'

'There's no cure,' he stated bluntly without turning round.

'I know, but there is treatment—steroids—and in this patient's case she responded well. I just feel the earlier these things are recognised. . .' She trailed off helplessly, miserably afraid that she might have undermined his authority but at the same time unrepentant if she had brought about an early diagnosis for Paula Cotton.

'I've already arranged for Paula to see a neurologist,' he said at last, still with his back to her.

'I know,' she replied quickly, 'she told me—maybe he would have found out. . .'

'And maybe he wouldn't,' he replied tersely, then he swung round to face her. 'All her tests were negative —you know that?'

'Yes, I know,' Alison replied calmly. 'But, as I said, SLE is extremely difficult to diagnose.'

'OK.' He nodded. 'I'll put your theory forward to the neurologist.'

'You'd do that?' She stared at him in surprise. She hadn't imagined for one moment he would.

'Of course,' he replied coolly. 'Didn't you think I would?'

She shrugged. 'I didn't think you'd be too happy at my diagnosing your patient.'

'Why?'

'Well, you didn't seem too happy at first about Brenda Dawson,' she retorted flatly.

He sighed. 'That was a different thing entirely— Brenda hadn't even given me a chance to show that I can be understanding—with Paula you have recently studied a very similar case. Besides, I'm not so arrogant as to assume that I know everything where my patients are concerned.'

'Brenda called in to see me again,' said Alison suddenly.

'Did she?' For a moment Grant looked surprised.

She nodded. 'Yes, she came to thank me for talking to you. She also said you'd been in to see her. That was good of you,' she added quietly.

He shrugged. 'It was the least I could do. I couldn't

have one of my patients thinking I was unapproachable over her problems.'

'You prescribed HRT for her?' Alison smiled.

'Yes, I also happen to be an advocate for it—between us I think we sorted things out for Brenda.' He paused and, leaning on her desk, looked into her face. 'Alison,' he went on gently, 'there are plenty of pitfalls in practice partnerships. This, however, is one of the compensations—being able to pool one's experiences and resources and not to be in hostile competition with each other. I feel we collaborated successfully over Brenda, I helped you with Ken Bridges, and now you've helped me with Paula—in fact, it's proving what I had begun to suspect.'

She looked up at him then and saw that he was smiling. 'Which is?'

'That you and I can work together and that we could form a very successful partnership.' As he spoke he leaned further forward and kissed first the tip of her nose then her lips in a long, lingering kiss.

It was at that precise moment that Gill opened the door and stuck her head round.

'Oh!' She looked dumbfounded. 'Oh!' she said again. 'You are in here. I was beginning to wonder. I thought. . .I thought. . .oh, I don't know what I thought!' Rolling her eyes, she backed out of the room and closed the door.

'I think we've shocked her.' Alison pulled a face.

'Oh, I don't know.' He grinned. 'I would imagine she'd be pleased—she and Hilda have been angling for this ever since you came back.'

'Well, I suspected Hilda had—but Gill as well? Are you sure?'

'Absolutely. I'm only happy we're able to give satisfaction.' He gave a complacent sigh.

'Grant. . .' Alison began warningly.

'All right. I know.' He grinned. 'Nothing's been settled yet and if we don't get on soon and do some work we won't have a practice to settle. I won't rush you, Alison, I promise, but we must talk. Things have changed now, haven't they?'

She sighed and nodded. 'Yes, Grant, they have changed, but let's keep this to ourselves just for the time being. . .'

'Very well. . .but not for too long. . .'

He went then, leaving her to her morning's patients, but later, after surgery as she shared a coffee with Gill, the secretary couldn't resist commenting.

'Was that what I thought it might be?' She jerked her head in the direction of Grant's surgery, her expression leaving Alison in no doubt as to what she meant.

'I don't know.' Deliberately Alison played for time, unwilling to incriminate herself too deeply. 'What did you think it might be?'

Gill was filing records in between taking sips of coffee, and she paused and peered at Alison over her glasses. 'Well, it looked to me like you and Dr Ashton were involved in a pretty heavy scene.'

'You watch too many American movies, Gill,' she replied flippantly.

Gill shrugged. 'Maybe I do.' It was a well-known fact at Fairacre that she was addicted to romantic films. 'But it doesn't alter what I saw. Does it?'

Alison smiled, curled her hands round her mug and sipped her coffee.

Gill was silent for a moment as she bent down to the lower shelf of records. Then, straightening up, she threw Alison a curious glance. 'Tell me,' she said, 'you and Dr Ashton—did you have something going between you some years ago?'

'I would imagine, Gill, that you know very well that we did. I dare say Hilda gave you all the details.'

'No, actually she didn't, Alison. Hilda never gossiped about you, Dr Kennedy, or Dr Ashton. But when you came home for your father's funeral, simply the way you and Dr Ashton looked at each other led me to draw my own conclusions. I asked Hilda then and she merely confirmed that you had been very close at one time.'

'It was a long time ago, Gill,' said Alison slowly.

'Maybe, but it doesn't look as if very much has changed,' observed Gill wryly.

Alison looked down into her mug, aware that her cheeks had grown warm. 'Things can never be quite the same as they were,' she muttered. 'People change —situations change.'

'True,' admitted Gill philosophically, then with a glint of mischief in her brown eyes added, 'but sometimes they can be even better the second time around —that is, if you're prepared to give them half a chance.'

'Honestly, Gill, I don't know why you and Hilda don't set up a dating agency—you'd make a fortune between you!' Shaking her head, Alison left Gill to answer the phone, which was ringing furiously, and made her way back to her consulting-room to prepare for her antenatal clinic.

Suddenly she had to get away from Gill, away from the speculation in her eyes, for she was afraid that if she stayed the conversation would escalate and she would end up admitting that things had gone a lot further between herself and Grant and that yes, it had been every bit as good if not better than she had remembered.

The rest of the week was busy, with very little opportunity for further discussion. Alison, slightly dazed by all that was happening, found herself experiencing little surges of pure joy when she was least expecting them. But in spite of that she still found that a part of her was holding back. She still loved Grant, she didn't doubt that now, and she longed to help him set up the plans he had for the practice—her doubting had nothing to do with that—rather it came from her own vulnerability, her daring to love again, to commit herself once more, while at the same time remembering just how hurt she'd been.

She promised herself that at the weekend she and Grant would find the time to talk so that her fears could be dispelled once and for all.

On Friday evening at the very end of the late evening surgery Alison saw that Cheryl Rossi had made an appointment to see her.

Cheryl sauntered into the surgery in her usual nonchalant fashion, but as she sat down and crossed her long legs Alison sensed an air of pent-up tension beneath the surface.

'What can I do for you, Cheryl?' she asked guardedly.

'Last time I saw you, I needed a repeat prescription for the Pill,' replied Cheryl coolly, coming straight to the point. 'You only gave me one packet. Your father used to give me six months' supply.'

'That's right,' Alison glanced down at Cheryl's notes. 'At the time I was only here in a temporary capacity.'

'Aren't you still?'

'I see from your records,' said Alison, choosing to ignore the question, 'that you had been experiencing some problems with the Pill—severe headaches and spotting between periods—and that Dr Kennedy had suggested that you may have to change brands or come off the Pill for a time and seek another form of contraceptive.'

'I wouldn't be keen to do that at this particular time.'

'Oh?' Alison glanced up and saw that Cheryl was studying her nails.

'I wouldn't want to risk a pregnancy.'

'Fair enough, but there are other methods—I'm sure we could find something acceptable. . .'

'I don't want to come off the Pill,' said Cheryl flatly.

'Would your husband object?'

'My husband?'

Something in Cheryl's tone made Alison look up again. 'Yes.' She nodded. 'I know some men object. . .but that still needn't be a problem, and your health must come first——'

'It's got nothing to do with my husband.'

'Oh?' Alison frowned. 'I don't understand.'

'Paul Rossi and I are separated—we're in the middle of a divorce.'

'Oh, I see. Well, in that case could you not——?'

'I'm in another relationship at the moment.' Her expression changed, became sly, and a warning bell sounded somewhere in Alison's brain. 'I shouldn't say really; it's all supposed to be hush-hush.' Cheryl leaned forward conspiratorially. 'Because of his position and the fact that my decree absolute won't be through for a few weeks, we have had to be utterly discreet, but——' she stared at Alison from under her eyelashes '—what the hell? You won't tell anyone because everything's confidential in here, isn't it?'

'Yes, Cheryl, that's correct, it is.' Alison took a deep breath. Suddenly she longed to get some fresh air. 'But you don't have to tell me anything, you know; it really isn't any of my business. I'm sure we can sort out your medication satisfactorily——'

'But I want to tell you,' Cheryl interrupted. 'I need to tell someone. The secrecy's driving me mad. I want to shout it from the rooftops—it's all so wonderful. You see, Alison, I've never felt this way about anyone before, and do you know what?' Her eyes widened. 'Grant says it's exactly the same for him.'

CHAPTER ELEVEN

'GRANT?' Alison hoped she sounded casual. 'Do you mean Dr Ashton?'

Cheryl was examining her nails again; Alison noticed that they were painted a bright cerise.

'Of course.' Cheryl looked up quickly then went on, 'But you mustn't say anything to him. You mustn't say anything to anyone, but especially not to him—he said no one must know until after my divorce—it would look bad for the practice. It seems incredible, I know——' she gave a little yawn, stifling it behind her hand '—but there are still a lot of awfully old-fashioned people in Woodbridge, and Grant feels they really wouldn't like their GP to be involved in any scandal. . . But afterwards—well, afterwards I can tell everyone. You didn't mind my telling you, did you?' Her eyes widened innocently. 'You know what it's like when you're in love—you want everyone to share it with you. I knew you'd be pleased for me, Alison; after all, we go back a long way, right back to that ghastly school.' She paused. 'And of course Grant and I go back quite a long way as well. . . We first went out together not long after Grant came to Woodbridge, even before I met Paul. . .and then, there's another reason why I thought you might be interested. . .' She paused again.

Unable to answer, afraid that her tongue might be

about to choke her, Alison raised her eyebrows.

'You see, Grant and I have only been able to meet in secret.' Cheryl gave her a sly little smile again. 'I don't know what we'd have done without your boat, *The Kittihawk*——'

'*The Kittihawk*?' Suddenly Alison found her voice.

'Yes, it's been a godsend—it was a bit close to my office of course, and Ken Bridges is so nosy—but we found a way.' She shrugged. 'They say love always finds a way, don't they?'

A mental picture of rumpled bed sheets in the cabin of *The Kittihawk* flew into her mind, then of Cheryl climbing down into the galley, hoisting herself on to the worktop and crossing her slim ankles, saying she would stay and talk to Grant.

Had Cheryl been there earlier and simply returned?

She blinked as she realised that Cheryl was talking again, and forced herself to concentrate.

'So now you see why I don't want to come off the Pill. I simply can't afford to take any risks at the present time.'

Taking a deep breath, Alison reached for her prescription pad. 'I'll give you a three-month supply of a different brand, then the position will need reviewing,' she said tersely.

'Right—I expect I'll have to see someone else then, won't I?' Cheryl stood up as Alison tore off the prescription and handed it to her.

'What makes you think that?' Levelly Alison met her gaze.

'Well, I dare say you'll be going back to Suffolk, won't you? Grant said he hoped you'd stay because it would be so much easier than trying to buy you out and finding another partner, but I expect you'll be glad to get away from this God-forsaken place.' She went then and for a long time Alison sat at her desk staring at the door, her thoughts in turmoil.

Then quite suddenly something inside her head seemed to snap and she stood up, clenching her fists. She marched to the door and wrenched it open. She would see him now. Confront him. Ask him what the hell he was playing at.

Then she stopped. She couldn't do that. Cheryl had made it quite plain that what she had told her had been in confidence. She was bound by the Hippocratic oath. If she broke that confidence, she had no doubt that Cheryl would have the book thrown at her.

Her heart was beating so rapidly that she felt as if her chest was about to burst. Returning to her desk, she sat down again and tried to get her emotions under control. Then with trembling fingers she pressed the number for Grant's intercom.

'Hello?' The sound of his voice, deep and unsuspecting, almost unnerved here and she was forced to take a deep breath.

'I have to go out, Grant,' she said. 'I won't be at home for dinner tonight.'

A surprised silence greeted her statement, then he said, 'Is everything all right, Alison?'

'Yes.'

'Anything I can do to help?'

'No, Grant—nothing.' Quickly she replaced the receiver, not giving him a chance to say more, then, grabbing her bag and her car keys, she hurried from the surgery, past a startled Gill, past the closed door of Grant's surgery where he obviously still had a patient, out of the house, and into her car.

She drove straight to the marina and was relieved to find that the chandlery was still open and that it was Ken Bridges in charge.

He looked surprised to see her.

'Hello, Ken. I want to buy a padlock for *The Kittihawk*,' she said tightly.

'A padlock? Yes, certainly.' He turned to a merchandise carousel behind him and lifted a packet from one of the racks.

'Are you worried about intruders?' He looked anxious.

'You could say that,' she replied tightly, and handed him a twenty-pound note.

He rang up the sale, then hesitated before handing her the change. 'Would you like me to fit it for you?' he asked quietly.

She looked up and met his gaze. 'Yes, please, Ken. Yes, I would.'

He opened the packet, slid one of the tiny keys on to the counter and handed it to her. 'I'll keep the other one till next time I see you.'

'Thanks, Ken.' She paused. 'Don't let anyone else have it, will you?'

'No, Alison.' His gaze held hers. 'Of course not.'

She turned to leave then paused, remembering. 'Oh, Ken, how is your back?'

'Much better, thanks. Grant's marvellous at the old manipulation.'

'Quite,' she replied tightly, then, not giving Ken a

chance to say any more, she hurried from the office.

She drove for miles—out of Woodbridge and into Yarmouth then round the coast to Freshwater and along the old Military Road that ran parallel to the sea.

The sun was sinking behind the horizon and a soft bank of sea mist was creeping inland, skimming the cliffs and hanging wraith-like over the marshes.

For once the peace and beauty of the scene failed to move her, and even when a barn owl rose out of a clump of hazel and flapped sedately towards a distant line of pine trees she hardly noticed. She felt hurt and betrayed and just wanted to be alone to get her tangled thoughts into some sort of order.

She met hardly any other traffic, just the occasional holiday-maker out for an evening drive, and at last she pulled off the road into a lay-by, switched off the engine and sat with her arms resting on the steering-wheel, staring out across the sea as Cheryl's words reverberated in her head.

Cheryl had made it quite plain that she and Grant had been sleeping together, which meant that he was two-timing them both. She had also made it plain that she had had some sort of relationship with him in the past—soon after he had come to Woodbridge, she had said, and if that was the case that would have been at the time that she and Grant had been so close. . . Alison felt a pain beneath her ribs even as she thought of it. Grant had told her that her father had tried to separate them because he thought her career would suffer. . .and she had believed him. . . Could the truth be that her father had known that Grant had been two-timing her and had tried to end the relationship to spare her pain? Had he seen through him? Known what he was like?

And what of Grant himself? Cheryl had implied that he was in love with her, but if that was so why had he tried to resume his relationship with her, Alison? Why had he wanted her to stay? Had it merely been to prove that he could get her back into bed again?

Her heart twisted again at the thought, then to add even further to her pain she recalled that Cheryl had said that Grant wanted her at Fairacre because it was easier than trying to buy her out and finding another partner. Surely it couldn't only be that?

Even as she tried to face the appalling possibility, another thought entered her mind. Grant himself had acknowledged her popularity in the town—the fact that she would attract patients, not only as a woman GP and an islander, but as her father's daughter. Was that another reason why he wanted her there—to attract business?

She couldn't work alongside him any longer. That much was certain. She couldn't stay in Woodbridge, in spite of her father's last wish.

Her father's last wish. . . That was still the puzzling part, the part that didn't quite fit. If her father had tried so hard to stop the relationship between herself and Grant, why had he changed his mind and done everything he could to bring them into partnership? Had it really only been because he wanted her to carry on the family tradition at Fairacre?

She sighed and rested her head on her hands.

It was a muddle, and probably she would never know the answers. The only thing she was certain about was the fact that she couldn't, and wouldn't, trust Grant Ashton ever again.

It was almost dusk when she finally started the engine and pulled back on to the road. She felt no better, but at least she now knew what she had to do.

To her relief Fairacre was in darkness when she returned and there was no sign of Grant's car.

She went straight upstairs and prepared for bed, then turned the key in the lock of her bedroom door and for safe measure propped a chair under the handle. She knew she would have to face Grant soon, knew there would be a showdown, but not tonight, she thought as she climbed into bed; tonight she felt exhausted and simply couldn't cope.

But in spite of her weariness sleep eluded her, and she was still awake when Grant's car swept up the drive. She heard him come into the house, go into the kitchen, then climb the stairs. She lay silent as she heard him try her door. Feigned sleep when he softly called her name. Heard him go to his own room, heard the click as he closed his door. Then with a sob she turned her face into her pillow.

She overslept, and when she came downstairs sunlight flooded the hall and the scent of honeysuckle drifted through the open door.

She found Gill in her office watering her plants.

'Just look at this African violet—isn't it beautiful? They usually die on me but this one has bloomed ever since I had it.' Gill looked up, then peered at Alison, her watering-can poised in mid-air. 'I say, are you all right, Alison? You look a bit peaky this morning.'

'I'm OK, Gill,' she replied. 'I didn't sleep very well, that's all.'

'Oh, I see.' Gill frowned. 'I haven't got your morning mail, I'm afraid. Dr Ashton picked it all up and took it into his room. He said he'd sort it out.'

'All right, Gill, thanks.' Slowly she made her way back to her consulting-room, only too aware of Gill's curiosity. She had barely entered her room when Grant tapped the open door and, pushing it fully open, entered the room behind her.

'Alison?' The question in his voice was only too apparent and when she turned she could see it repeated in his eyes.

'Yes, Grant?' She tried to sound businesslike, matter-of-fact, and let her gaze flicker from his face to the pile of letters in his hand.

'I've brought your post. . .'

'Thank you.' She took it and turned away.

'Alison. . .!'

'Yes?'

'What's wrong?'

'Nothing.'

'I thought——'

'Was there anything else, Grant?' Abruptly she interrupted him. 'I must get on. I overslept and I need to catch up.'

'Of course.' He hesitated, clearly ill at ease. 'I thought you might like to know I've had a letter about Paula Cotton.'

'Oh?' She was interested—relieved to discuss an issue that wasn't personal.

'Yes, it rather looks as if you were right. The neurologist thinks there is a decided possibility of SLE.'

'Poor Paula—it doesn't look as if she'll ever have the baby they so longed for.'

'Maybe not, although it has been known, apparently, but even if she can't have a child she has her life, and thanks to you the proper treatment can start immediately and give her relief from her symptoms.'

'It was only a matter of time before you diagnosed it.' She shrugged.

'You were more familiar with the condition than I. But that's the beauty of a partnership, Alison.' He paused and she found herself holding her breath. 'We can help each other.'

She remained silent, staring at the floor.

'Alison?' he said quietly. 'There is something wrong. I want to know what it is.'

'I don't want there to be any partnership, Grant,' she said at last.

'What?' The exclamation was low so that Gill wouldn't hear, but it nevertheless registered his shock.

She was aware that he was staring at her but she couldn't bring herself to meet his gaze.

'I'm sorry, Grant,' she said, 'but there it is.'

'But I don't understand. Why?'

'I just don't think it would work, that's all.' She shook her head. 'I've come to the conclusion that you can't turn the clock back. Too much changes with the passing of time.'

He continued to stare at her. 'I don't understand you, Alison,' he said tightly. 'You need to make up your mind exactly what it is you want out of life.'

She was saved from answering by the sharp buzz of

the intercom. She walked to the desk and lifted the receiver.

'There's an emergency for Dr Ashton,' said Gill. 'A patient with a suspected heart attack.'

'OK, Gill, he's here.' She handed the phone to Grant, who took it and listened to what Gill had to tell him.

'All right, Gill,' he said. 'Tell them I'm on my way.'

He replaced the receiver and looked long and hard at Alison, then abruptly he turned and strode from the room.

As she watched him go she felt as if her heart was breaking.

Somehow she got through the rest of the day, thankful that it was Saturday and there weren't so many surgeries.

She knew that she and Grant would have to talk further to discuss the future of the practice, and she found herself dreading the prospect so much that she decided it might be a good idea to talk it through with Godfrey Warner first. When she phoned to speak to him, however, she was told that he was at a conference on the mainland and wouldn't be back until the following day.

She sighed and stretched, pushing her hair back from her face. Gill had gone home and she was on call. She hadn't seen Grant since before lunch when he'd gone out to do his house calls. It had been his afternoon off and she wondered if he had gone to *The Kittihawk* —if he had, he would have been in for a shock, she thought grimly. As she stood up and flexed her muscles the phone rang, its unexpectedness making her jump. Wearily she picked up the receiver.

'Dr Kennedy speaking.'

'Hello, Doctor. It's Newport Police Station. Sergeant Jones.'

'Hello, Sergeant—how can I help you?'

'There's been a fire reported in your area—the brigade have radioed in to ask for medical assistance. We have ambulance crews on the way but we would like a doctor in attendance as well.'

'Of course. Where is the fire?'

'It's a place called Marine Court. Apparently it's a block of retirement flats——'

'Yes, I know it—I'm on my way,' said Alison.

Pausing only to check her medical case, she locked the surgery, grabbed her mobile phone and ran to her car. It took her less than ten minutes to drive to Marine Court and when she arrived she found one fire engine in attendance and another approaching from the opposite direction. Two police cars had also arrived and one uniformed officer was directing the traffic while another was trying to calm the little groups of people who stood in the street.

As she hurried from the car towards the entrance of the flats she looked up and saw smoke billowing from several upstairs windows. Sirens screamed and wailed in the distance and an acrid, pungent smell filled the air.

'Where do you think you're going, miss?' A stocky figure in the uniform of the chief fire officer barred her path.

'I'm Dr Kennedy,' she explained. 'The police

contacted me for assistance.' She glanced anxiously up at the building. 'Is there anyone still in there?'

The chief nodded. 'Yes, we believe there are at least two residents inside.'

'Then maybe I should try and get to them...' Alison began to move forward but he put out his arm, restraining her.

'No, Doctor. I'm sorry, I can't allow you to go in there.'

'But——'

'One doctor is quite enough.'

'What do you mean?' She frowned.

'A Dr Ashton is already inside.'

'What?' She stared at him, then a roaring noise filled the air followed by the sound of shattering glass and they both instinctively drew back as an upstairs window blew out, sending glass showering over the pavement. At the same moment wicked tongues of flame leapt up the side of the building. There were shouts from other members of the fire crew as they moved in, while the police began moving the occupants of the flats and other members of the public to a safer area.

'Did you say Dr Ashton was in there?' Alison caught the man's arm as he would have moved away.

'Apparently so. He arrived before we did and went straight in. It seems the fire started in the cloakroom of a flat on the second floor and we think the two occupants of that flat are still in there—a man by the name of Attrill and his wife.'

'Seth?' Alison looked up at the building again.

'You know them?'

'Yes. Oh yes.' Wildly she stared up at the second-floor flat. Grant was in there with Seth and Mabel. Dear God. . .please. . .

'Are you a doctor?' A young policeman caught at her arm.

'Yes. . .what is it?'

'A couple of people over there need help.' He pointed to the marina offices. Quickly Alison sped across the forecourt while the fire chief began issuing orders to his crew.

Inside the offices Alison found Ken Bridges helping the police, who had brought in several of the elderly residents who were suffering from smoke inhalation and shock.

Moments later two ambulances carrying oxygen equipment arrived. Alison moved swiftly from patient to patient, administering oxygen and checking for injuries.

When she had satisfied herself that no one was in any immediate danger, she left them in the charge of the paramedics and hurried back to the forecourt.

By this time more and more flames could be seen leaping from the living-room of Seth's flat, while a fire-tender had moved into position and a turntable ladder with a hydraulic rescue platform was being elevated to the balcony.

As she watched in growing horror a figure appeared on the balcony and she realised it was Seth. Amid much confusion, and seemingly some reluctance on Seth's part, he was persuaded on to the platform, then the fire officer assisting him called down to his colleagues that there were still more persons inside the flat, one of whom was in bad shape.

In an agony of suspense Alison watched as Seth was lowered to the ground and helped from the platform, which was immediately elevated again.

Automatically she hurried to Seth, crouching beside him on the ground as he coughed and gasped for breath.

'It's all right, Seth.' She signalled to one of the paramedics for oxygen.

His face blackened from smoke, his eyes red-rimmed and sore, Seth recognised her in spite of his anguish.

'Mabel. . .' he gasped. 'Mabel's still in there. . .it's her asthma. . .she can't breathe.'

'Take it easy, Seth, she'll be all right. They'll get her out. Dr Ashton. . .?'

'He's with her. . .' Seth nodded. 'He were marvellous. . .' He gasped again, then slumped in relief as Alison placed the oxygen mask over his face. Then she noticed his hands.

She stood up and signalled to the ambulance driver. 'This man has severe burns to his hands,' she said as she rummaged in her case for Flamazine cream. 'I'll put this on to cool the burning,' she explained, 'and I'll give him an injection to help ease the pain, then I'd like you to get him to hospital as soon as possible.'

Moments later she watched as the ambulance bearing Seth pulled out of the forecourt, then, with her heart full of dread, she turned back to the flats.

The fire officer had climbed off the platform and had disappeared inside the bedroom. The balcony appeared to be empty, although through the smoke it was difficult to be sure. Alison found herself praying that Mabel was still alive and that Grant would get out unharmed.

As she waited for what seemed like an eternity she was joined by Ken Bridges.

'He'll be OK, Alison,' he said quietly, so quietly that no one else heard.

'I hope so, Ken,' she replied. 'Oh, I hope so.' She swallowed, fighting back tears. 'If anything happens to him. . .'

'I know,' he replied gently. 'I know. . .' Then he clutched her arm. 'Look!' He pointed. 'Something's happening!'

Figures had appeared on the balcony, but the smoke had thickened and it was still difficult to see what was happening and to distinguish who was who.

Then, with a great surge of relief, Alison realised that one of the figures was Grant and that he and the fireman had carried a third figure, presumably Mabel, out of the flat.

Even as the crowd below watched, the pair on the balcony managed to get Mabel on to the platform, but as the fireman joined her and the platform swung away there was a cry from someone in the crowd.

'The curtains are alight!'

'Look! The bedroom's on fire now!'

Helplessly Alison watched as Grant appeared to be trapped on the balcony while the fire raged behind him.

Then, just when it seemed that all was lost and he would be caught up in the flames, the platform swung back. Grant climbed on to the balcony rail and stood there, poised, and as a gasp went up from the crowd he launched himself forward and caught hold of the sides of the platform. It swung out again with Grant grasping the rails and a great sigh of relief rose from the crowd.

After that it was only a matter of seconds before the platform was lowered to the ground.

With a sob Alison started forward and as Grant reached the ground he turned and almost fell into her open arms.

'Oh, Grant!' she gasped. 'Thank God you're safe!' desperately she held him close.

'It's all right,' he murmured against her hair. 'It's all right, Alison.'

But for a moment she couldn't let him go, could only hold him against her in relief, then she leaned her head back and looked at him, taking in his grimy face, streaked with sweat, and his dishevelled hair. 'Thank God!' she whispered again.

CHAPTER TWELVE

MABEL was still unconscious when she was lifted into the ambulance, but her breathing, with the aid of an oxygen mask, was not so laboured. By this time the fire crews had the fire under control, and as the crowd began to disperse Alison turned to Grant, who was sitting on the kerb by the roadside with Ken Bridges' jacket round his shoulders.

'Come on,' she said, indicating the open doors of the waiting ambulance. 'You go with them—I'll follow in my car.'

'There's no need for that——' Grant began, but she cut him short.

'There's every need. You've inhaled a lot of smoke. Don't argue; you're going to Casualty and that's that.'

'But. . .' A paroxysm of coughing seized Grant, putting paid to any further protest, and with a shrug he allowed a paramedic to assist him into the ambulance.

Barely twenty minutes later they reached the hospital and Alison watched as Mabel and Grant were whisked away into Casualty.

'Will you wait?' asked the casualty sister, who knew Alison slightly.

'Yes, I'd better—Dr Ashton doesn't have transport —I shouldn't imagine he'll be too long.'

'I wouldn't have thought so either,' the sister agreed. 'Perhaps you'd like a cup of tea while you're waiting?'

'I think what I will do,' Alison replied, 'is go up to Orthopaedics and see my friend Hilda Lloyd—she may hear rumours about Dr Ashton being in a fire and will worry about him.'

Hilda was sitting up in bed working on a piece of cross-stitch embroidery.

She looked up in surprise as Alison approached. 'Hello, love,' she said. 'I didn't expect to see you today.'

'I didn't expect to be here, Hilda.' Alison sat down beside the bed. 'How are you feeling?'

'I'm doing very well—better each day, but——' Hilda frowned at her over her glasses '—you look pale, Alison; what is it? There's something wrong, isn't there?'

Alison took a deep breath. 'There's nothing for you to worry about, Hilda, but there has been a fire.'

'A fire!' Alarm flickered in Hilda's blue eyes. 'At Fairacre?'

'No, not at Fairacre,' she replied quickly, 'at Marine Court. It seems it started in Seth and Mabel Attrill's flat.'

'Are they all right?' Hilda's eyes widened with shock and she set her embroidery down on the bedspread.

'They've been brought in,' Alison said gently, then went on, 'Seth has burnt his hands and Mabel is having difficulty with her breathing. They both inhaled a lot of smoke. . .' She hesitated. 'Anyway they are in Casualty now. . .and so is Dr Ashton,' she added at last.

'Dr Ashton! What did he have to do with it?' Hilda struggled to sit up and winced with sudden pain.

'He rescued them, Hilda,' said Alison quietly. 'That's what I came to tell you—I didn't want you hearing it from anyone else.'

'But is he all right?'

'Hopefully, yes.'

'Well——' Hilda leaned weakly back against her pillows '—thank goodness for that. I couldn't bear it if anything happened to Dr Ashton as well.'

'He's very special to you, isn't he, Hilda?' said Alison gently.

'Yes, he is—almost as special as you. . .' she nodded, then hesitated. 'Is he special to you again, Alison?' she asked, and the anxiety in her voice was only too obvious.

'Why do you ask that?' Alison looked up sharply.

'I don't know—there was just something about the way you said his name just now—almost as if you were as relieved as me that he hadn't come to any harm.'

'Well, of course I'm glad he isn't injured,' Alison replied. 'But that's about as far as it goes, Hilda,' she added firmly.

'Oh—I am disappointed. . .' Hilda's face fell.

'In fact, Hilda,' Alison intervened swiftly, 'I hadn't intended telling you this yet, but, since we're on the subject, I'm sorry, but I shall soon be making arrangements to go back to Suffolk.'

'Oh, Alison love——' Hilda stared up at her in dismay '—I had hoped. . .'

'I know and I'm sorry, but that's the way it is—there can't ever be anything between Grant and me again. Now——' she stood up '—I suppose I'd better get back to Casualty and see what's happening.' She looked down but Hilda didn't appear to be listening to her.

'He would have been sorry too, that his plan hasn't come to anything.' Hilda's muttering was almost to herself.

'What do you mean?' Alison frowned. 'You're not going to start talking in riddles again, are you, Hilda?'

'No.' Hilda sighed. 'There's no point any more.'

'So what did you mean about a plan? Whose plan?'

'Your father's, of course,' Hilda stared up at her in mild exasperation and when Alison's look remained blank she added, 'Concerning the partnership.'

'The partnership? You mean you knew all about that? My father discussed it with you?'

'No, I didn't know anything at the time——' Hilda shook her head '—but since then I've put two and two together and realised what your father had done and why he'd done it.'

'Well, perhaps you'd care to enlighten me—because I would dearly like to know why he apparently took such pains to break Grant and me up——'

'It was for your own good, dear, your career——'

'—only to go to such lengths to bring us together again. It doesn't make sense—he might have known it would have been a tremendous strain living and working together after what had happened in the past.'

Hilda was silent for a moment then quietly she said, 'Alison, your father once told me he felt guilty for coming between you two because in all his years he had never seen a couple so much in love.'

Alison stared at her in astonishment. 'He said that...!'

'Yes, and he also said it was his dearest wish to somehow make amends. I didn't know what he intended to do, neither did I know he was so ill. . . but afterwards, when it was all over and I learnt about the partnership, I knew it was his way of trying to make amends and bring you back together again.' She peered anxiously up at Alison. 'Are you absolutely certain, dear, that there's no chance. . .?'

'Absolutely, Hilda,' Alison replied firmly. 'I'm sorry, but I can't trust him, and if you don't have trust you have very little else.'

Hilda sighed. 'He always appears a most trustworthy sort of person to me. . .'

'Hilda, you don't understand; there's a lot more to it than you know. . .but I really must stop gossiping and get myself back to Woodbridge—no doubt news of the fire will have got round and the phone won't stop ringing this evening.'

She finally took her leave of Hilda, but as she travelled back to the ground floor of the hospital in the lift Alison couldn't prevent a pang as she thought of what Hilda had just told her.

At last she knew what had motivated her father in setting up the partnership, and deep inside she was glad that it hadn't simply been because he wanted a Kennedy at Fairacre. The only pity was that his good intentions had come too late and were in vain.

When she reached Casualty it was to find Grant ready and waiting for her to take him home.

'Have you had a check-up?' she asked briskly, trying to ignore the expression in his eyes.

'Yes, Doctor.'

'Was everything all right?'

'Yes, Doctor.' He grinned. 'And I've even had a chest X-ray just to be on the safe side.'

'I'm glad to hear it.' She tried to act matter-of-factly but she was conscious that he was staring at her in a very intimate way.

'Have you heard anything about Mabel?' she asked in the same brisk tone.

'She's still in a rather bad way, but I think we were in time.'

'Good, and Seth?'

'He's been warded for the moment,' Grant replied, 'but apparently he's waiting to be transferred to the burns unit at Odstock. I thought you might want to see him before we go home.' He stood back for her to precede him through the double swing doors.

'Good idea,' she said. As she brushed past him she caught the smell of burning which still lingered on his clothes and hair, and she was reminded just how close to death he himself had been.

On their way to the ward she remained silent, but she was only too aware of a growing tension between them, as if Grant was about to say something. In a moment of rising panic, and not giving him the chance to speak, she said quickly, 'I've just been to see Hilda —I wanted to tell her about the fire in case someone else did—I knew she would only worry about you being there.' She threw him a curious glance. 'As a matter of interest,' she asked, 'how did you come to be at the flats?'

'I had been to the marina.'

The marina. He'd been to *The Kittihawk*. She swallowed and looked away.

'I was on my way home,' he went on, 'when I saw the smoke. Someone had already phoned the fire station. Someone else said there were people inside.'

'Does anyone know how it started?' asked Alison uneasily.

'Not exactly.'

'What do you mean, not exactly?' She frowned as a doubt that had been niggling at the back of her mind for the past few hours began to become a distinct possibility.

'Well, Seth was babbling on about it being his pipe that had caused it, but——' Grant shook his head '—I don't know. . .'

'I hope I haven't inadvertently been responsible.' Alison bit her lip.

'You?' Grant glanced sideways at her and frowned. 'I don't understand; why should it have anything to do with you?'

'Well, when I saw Mabel recently she was in such a state with her asthma that I mentioned to Seth that he shouldn't smoke his pipe in the same room as her. I suggested that he could smoke on the balcony. The fire chief said they thought the fire had started in the Attrills' cloakroom—maybe Seth was smoking in there. . .?'

'No, I don't think it was that,' replied Grant slowly. 'I didn't take a lot of notice at the time because I was more concerned with Mabel, but Seth was going on that he had been out on the balcony having a smoke, and when he came in he put his pipe into his jacket pocket, then hung his jacket up in the cloakroom. I can only assume the pipe was still alight.'

'Oh, God!' Frantically Alison ran her fingers through her hair, looping it back behind one ear. 'If I hadn't told him to alter his habits this probably wouldn't have happened.'

'It wasn't your fault,' Grant said firmly. 'You were acting in Mabel's best interests. Seth should have made sure the pipe was out. It must have smouldered for some time before setting light to the jacket then to the other coats in the cloakroom.'

By this time they had reached the entrance to the ward and Grant paused, one hand on the swing door.

'I had a devil of a job to get in to them,' he said quietly. 'Mabel was in a bad way even then and Seth had burnt his hands trying to put the fire out. The living-room was ablaze and it was impossible to get them out—I had to get them into the bedroom. I guessed the fire crews would use the bedroom balcony as a means of escape.'

'All I can say,' said Alison as Grant finally pushed open the door, 'is that it was a good job you were in the vicinity.'

'I'd been to *The Kittihawk*,' he said as they began to walk down the ward.

'I guessed as much.'

'I couldn't get in, of course.'

'No, you wouldn't,' she replied evenly.

He didn't answer as by that time they had reached a small ante-room at the far end of the ward.

Seth was dressed and sitting in an easy-chair, his

hands heavily bandaged. He was staring out of the window and didn't turn round as Alison and Grant came into the room.

'Hello, Seth,' Alison said quietly, moving round in front of him.

It seemed to take a moment for him to focus, to realise who she was, then he nodded slightly and his gaze flickered to Grant.

'How are you feeling now?' Grant drew a chair forward for Alison while he perched on the edge of the bed.

'Not so bad,' Seth replied shortly, then fell silent again.

'I understand you're going to Odstock,' Alison said, and when he merely nodded in reply she added, 'They have a very fine burns unit there.'

'Skin grafts,' he said morosely.

'Yes, so I understand,' Alison replied, then positively she added, 'They can do so much these days, Seth.'

He didn't reply, his attitude suggesting that he was unconvinced, then quite suddenly he said, 'Do you know how Mabel is?'

Alison hesitated and it was Grant who replied. 'She's as well as can be expected, Seth, but you have to remember she's been through a very traumatic time— we all have, but in Mabel's case. . .well, it's worse for her because of her chest. She's in good hands here, though,' he added gently.

Seth grunted and made no further comment but Alison noticed that his eyes were bright with unshed tears.

'I'm sure she'll be all right, Seth.' She leaned forward and lightly touched his arm.

'But it were all my fault—weren't it?' He looked up helplessly, and as Alison saw the anguish in his expression her heart went out to him.

'It was an accident, Seth,' she said firmly.

'I was trying to do what you said. . .you know, not smoking in the same room and all that. I was out on the balcony and the phone rang. I came in quick, like, to answer it and I stuffed me pipe in me pocket—I suppose I just weren't thinking. When I smoke indoors, I always rest the pipe against the rim of the ashtray when I've finished—then it don't matter if it's not quite out—but this time. . .this time it were different. . .' He trailed off and a tear trickled down his cheek. He made as if to raise his hand, then remembered his dressings and gave a helpless little shrug.

Alison took a tissue from a box on the locker and, leaning forward, wiped his face.

They sat with him for several more minutes then at last, with a promise to visit Mabel again in a few days' time, they stood up and prepared to go. As they reached the door, however, Seth spoke again.

'I tell you one thing.' He spoke as if they hadn't already said goodbye.

'What's that, Seth?' Alison paused, one hand on the door-handle.

'I'm never going to smoke again.'

'I'm glad to hear it,' Alison replied firmly, while Grant gave a soft chuckle.

'I mean it. I don't want to see another pipe as long as I live. And I tell you another thing; if it weren't for you, Dr Ashton, I don't know where we would be. A hero—that's what you were.' He glanced at Alison. 'I'm telling you, Alison, he's a hero and no mistake.'

They were mostly silent on the drive home and by the time they reached Fairacre it was almost dusk, a soft twilight that seemed to steal in across the estuary and settle over the marshes. They sat for a while watching tiny pipistrelle bats dart back and forth between the house and the tall fir trees that lined the drive. In the end it was Grant who broke the silence.

'You know something?' he said softly. 'When I stepped off that platform and found you waiting for me I could have sworn there was love in your eyes.'

'I was relieved you were safe,' she said quickly.

'Only relieved?' He raised his eyebrows and she looked away, unable to cope with the expression in his eyes.

'Anyone would have been relieved...' she protested.

'I thought, just for one crazy moment, that I had been imagining the coolness between us, that everything was back the way it's been the last few days.' Gently he lifted her hand from the steering-wheel and, turning it over, began caressing her palm with his thumb.

Instinctively she stiffened and drew in her breath. She couldn't cope with this...with his nearness, the look in his eyes, his touch. If she was going to go through with her decision to leave Fairacre, to leave him, then she could have no further contact with him. Desperately she tried to pull away, to get out of the car, but he tightened his grip on her hand.

'Alison,' he said softly.

'No, Grant. No. I told you before, as far as I'm concerned it's over between us.'

'I can't believe that—I think you love me.'

'I can't trust you, Grant, and I can't love someone I don't trust.'

'Supposing you found that you could, after all, trust me—would that make a difference?'

'I don't see how——'

'Supposing I were to tell you,' he went on quietly, relentlessly, 'that I was so puzzled by your sudden change of heart that I decided to find out what had caused it?'

'What do you mean?' She frowned.

'Think about it, Alison. During the last week we had become almost as close as it's possible for two people to be. When we made love there were no barriers, no inhibition sex was glorious between us.'

She couldn't contradict him, knowing that what he said was the truth, but she felt the ready colour touch her cheeks as she acknowledged it.

When she remained silent, he went on, 'Our love seemed to grow, our plans for the future seemed to be taking shape, then suddenly it all changed. I couldn't believe it at first, couldn't understand why, then I tried to reason it out and came to the conclusion that something must have happened to make you change your mind.'

Still she didn't answer, neither confirming nor denying his conclusions.

'I needed time to think back to what it might have been,' he continued, 'so I went down to the marina to do some work on *The Kittihawk*. When I got there I found it padlocked.' He paused and glanced at her. 'I thought it strange that you hadn't mentioned it, especially as you knew I had been working on the boat, so I went across to the office and found Ken Bridges. I asked him if he knew anything about it. He told me you had bought the padlock from him and that he had offered to fit it for you. I asked if he had a key, and he said you had told him he wasn't to give a key to anyone else and he presumed that included me.'

Still Alison remained silent.

'I asked Ken if he knew why, and he said he didn't know for sure, but that he wouldn't be surprised if you weren't sick to death of Cheryl Rossi hanging around.' He paused again and Alison turned her head and looked out of the window, then she felt his hand on her chin as gently he turned her face to his.

'Are you, Alison?' he asked softly at last. 'Are you sick of Cheryl? Did you put the padlock on to keep her off *The Kittihawk*?'

'Ken had no right to make assumptions like that.' She shook her head. 'Cheryl Rossi is my patient. . .'

'I know that. I also know she came to see you last evening.'

'How?'

'How? Simply because I saw her come out of your room, that's all, Alison,' he replied gently. 'I hadn't thought anything of it at the time.'

She bit her lip and tried to turn away.

'You had been fine before last night's surgery. It was only afterwards that you began acting strangely towards me. After finding the padlock on *The*

Kittihawk, then talking to Ken Bridges, I began to put two and two together...'

'Grant, I'm sorry but I can't——'

'Betray a confidence?' he finished for her.

'You wouldn't—would you?' she demanded, then, not giving him a chance to answer, she went on, 'You wouldn't even betray my father's confidence to me, even when you knew he was so ill.'

'No, Alison, that's quite correct, I wouldn't, and I wouldn't expect you to do so either. But in this case you don't need to.'

'I don't understand.' She stared at him. 'What do you mean?'

'After speaking to Ken, I went to see Cheryl—she lives on the far side of the marina.'

'Oh, God, I hope she didn't think...'

'No, Alison, she doesn't think anything of the sort. I don't know exactly what Cheryl told you, but I gather she may have given you the impression that she and I have something going between us. No——' he held up his other hand as Alison opened her mouth to say something '——you don't have to answer that. Cheryl admitted as much. Now I want you to hear the correct version.'

She tensed, waiting for him to go on, bracing herself against what she might be about to hear.

'I have taken Cheryl out on a few occasions in the past,' he admitted. 'The first time was to a Medical Association dinner when you were at medical school. I didn't have a partner and your father arranged for Cheryl to accompany me.'

'My father!' She threw him a startled glance.

'Yes.' His expression tightened. 'Apparently he knew Cheryl's father—played golf with him, I believe. Anyway, I guess at the time it was all part of the ploy to keep us apart,' he added grimly. 'After we'd split up I saw her perhaps a couple more times, then she met, and later married, Paul Rossi.'

He paused, but continued caressing the palm of her hand. 'Recently,' he went on at last, 'I heard that she and Rossi were getting divorced. I wasn't particularly surprised; I never did think it would last—Cheryl's too flighty.' He took a deep breath. 'When I began working on *The Kittihawk*, Cheryl got into the habit of visiting me, usually during her lunch-hour. We would sometimes share a sandwich and a drink.'

'And that was all?' Alison raised her eyebrows, unable to get the image of the rumpled bedclothes out of her mind.

'Absolutely.' He was emphatic. 'Cheryl had hinted that she would have liked more to come of it.'

'And how did you feel about that?'

'At first I was indifferent. I didn't particularly want to get involved with her—I'd heard that her divorce had been pretty messy—I didn't mind talking to her, or even having the occasional drink, but that was as far as it went, and that was before you came home, Alison.' His green eyes darkened. 'When you arrived, everything changed. Cheryl knew it as well, just as she knew that in the past you and I had meant a lot to one another.'

'She certainly seemed to know a lot about me and the set-up here,' said Alison carefully.

'I suppose she made it her business to find out—

that probably wasn't difficult. Gossip and speculation has been rife in the town since you came back.'

'She also made a frequent point of wanting to know when I was going back to Suffolk,' Alison commented drily.

'She probably thought that if you went away again I might feel differently about her. Alison——' Grant turned to face her in the confined space of the front seats of the car '—there's nothing between Cheryl Rossi and myself. Please believe me.'

She sighed. She so wanted to believe him but she still felt very vulnerable. Gradually she allowed her eyes to meet his.

'I love you, Alison,' he said simply. 'I want you to marry me.'

For one moment she thought he was joking, but his expression was serious and quite suddenly her heart was doing crazy things as she stared at him.

'What do you say?' A hint of amusement entered the green eyes.

'So you don't just want me to help you run the surgery because I'm the easiest option?' Her voice, when she found it, was husky with emotion.

Lifting his hands, he cupped her face. 'I do want you to help me run the surgery—I think we would make a great medical team—but more than that, much more than that, I want you beside me as my wife. Will you trust me again, Alison?'

They stared at each other for a long moment, then Grant kissed the tip of her nose before opening the car door. 'I think,' he said softly, 'you may need a little more convincing that I mean what I say.'

As they entered the house Grant turned and locked the front door, shutting out the world.

'I'll take all the convincing you're prepared to give——' Alison chuckled as he turned his smoke-blackened face towards her again '—on one condition.'

'Which is?'

'That you have a shower first.'

He glanced in the hall mirror, then pulled a face as he caught sight of his appearance.

'Good grief, I look like a chimney sweep,' he laughed. 'I'll take a shower—but also on one condition.'

She raised her eyebrows.

'That you take one with me.'

The moon had risen over the estuary when much later they strolled through the coppice. Their feet made no sound on the soft ground, the only noises being the rustlings of birds and wildlife in the undergrowth, and the occasional snapping of a twig.

In the soft summer darkness the moonlight filtered through the trees, lighting the contours of Alison's face as she lifted it for Grant's kiss.

When at last, with a sigh, they finally drew apart she rested her head against his chest and said, 'Tomorrow we must go and tell Hilda—I think she should be the first to know.'

'Of course,' he murmured against her hair.

'She'll be so pleased. Do you know, Grant,' she said after a moment, 'that Hilda told me today that my father had told her he felt guilty at parting us and that he wanted to make amends? When she heard about the partnership she knew it was his way of trying to put things right. . . Fancy Hilda knowing that and not saying anything.'

He didn't answer, remaining very still.

She lifted her head and looked up at him. 'Grant? Did you hear what I said? I said——'

'Yes, I know.' He smiled down at her and in the moonlight she saw a glint in his eyes. 'You said fancy Hilda not saying anything—but that's not strictly true. . .'

'What do you mean, not true?'

'Well, she may not have said anything to you—but she did to me. . .'

'What? What do you mean? What did she say to you?'

'She told me that your father had said he felt guilty about parting us and that he wanted to make amends.'

'But you said the partnership had come as much of a shock to you as it had to me. . .'

'That's quite true, it had—Hilda didn't tell me that until after you had come back for our six-month trial.'

'So why didn't you say anything to me?' she demanded.

'Would it have made any difference if I had?' When she merely shrugged, he laughed, hugged her and added, 'Besides, how could I? By that time I too was hoping. . .but you had made it quite plain that you wanted our relationship to be strictly professional. . .'

For a long moment she stared up at him in the darkness, then she realised he was laughing.

'Grant Ashton—you're impossible! I really think you could have——' she began to protest helplessly but swiftly he silenced her with yet another kiss, then, when at last he released her, she said, 'Just for that I've decided not to sell you *The Kittihawk*...'

'You mean you've considered it?'

'I had.'

'I'm devastated.' He kissed her again. 'Won't you change your mind?'

'No. I'm sorry, Grant—there's absolutely no way I can sell *The Kittihawk*, because I've decided to give it away.'

'What?'

'Yes, it's to be a wedding present to my future husband.'

He gave a gasp and she laughed softly. 'But once again there's a condition.'

'Which is?'

'When I want to sail, he'll take me wherever I want to go.'

'I can't imagine that will prove to be a problem,' he murmured, then, lowering his head, once again covered her mouth with his.

MILLS & BOON

Christmas Treasures

Unwrap the romance this Christmas

Four exciting new Romances by favourite Mills & Boon authors especially for you this Christmas.

A Christmas Wish - Betty Neels
Always Christmas - Eva Rutland
Reform Of The Rake - Catherine George
Christmas Masquerade - Debbie Macomber

Published: November 1994

Available from WH Smith, John Menzies, Volume One, Forbuoys, Martins, Woolworths, Tesco, Asda, Safeway and other paperback stockists.

SPECIAL PRICE : £5.70
(4 BOOKS FOR THE PRICE OF 3)

Cruel Legacy

PENNY JORDAN

Cruel Legacy

When tragedy strikes, the wounds are deep and irrevocable

One man's untimely death deprives a wife of her husband, robs a man of his job and offers someone else the chance of a lifetime...

Suicide — the only way out for Andrew Ryecart, facing crippling debt. An end to his troubles, but for those he leaves behind the problems are just beginning, as the repercussions of this most desperate of acts reach out and touch the lives of six different people — changing them forever.

Special large-format paperback edition

**OCTOBER
£8.99**

W⊕RLDWIDE

Available from WH Smith, John Menzies, Volume One, Forbuoys, Martins, Woolworths, Tesco, Asda, Safeway and other paperback stockists.

NORA ROBERTS

SWEET REVENGE

Adrianne's glittering lifestyle was the perfect foil for her extraordinary talents — no one knew her as *The Shadow*, the most notorious jewel thief of the decade. She had a secret ambition to carry out the ultimate heist — one that would even an old and bitter score. But she would need all her stealth and cunning to pull it off, with Philip Chamberlain, Interpol's toughest and smartest cop, hot on her trail. His only mistake was to fall under Adrianne's seductive spell.

AVAILABLE NOW   **PRICE £4.99**

WORLDWIDE

Available from WH Smith, John Menzies, Volume One, Forbuoys, Martins, Woolworths, Tesco, Asda, Safeway and other paperback stockists.

MILLS & BOON

LOVE ON CALL

The books for enjoyment this month are:

NOTHING LEFT TO GIVE Caroline Anderson
HIS SHELTERING ARMS Judith Ansell
CALMER WATERS Abigail Gordon
STRICTLY PROFESSIONAL Laura MacDonald

♥ ♥ ♥ ♥ ♥ ♥

Treats in store!

Watch next month for the following absorbing stories:

LAKESIDE HOSPITAL Margaret Barker
A FATHER'S LOVE Lilian Darcy
PASSIONATE ENEMIES Sonia Deane
BURNOUT Mary Hawkins

Available from W.H. Smith, John Menzies, Volume One, Forbuoys, Martins, Tesco, Asda, Safeway and other paperback stockists.

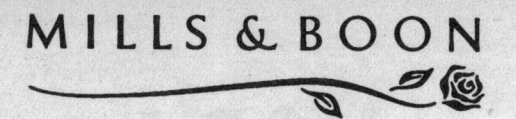

Also available from Mills & Boon Reader Service, Freepost, P.O. Box 236, Croydon, Surrey CR9 9EL.

Readers in South Africa - write to:
Book Services International Ltd, P.O. Box 41654, Craighall, Transvaal 2024.